DIRTY TALK, BOOKS 3 & 4

OPAL CAREW

Dirty Talk, Books 3 & 4
Opal Carew

Sonny has a debilitating fear of men.
Tal is a scary looking tattooed bad-ass.
Can Tal get Sonny past her fear
and help her become whole?

Sonny is terrified of men, but there's something about Tal that allows her to open up to him and her trust for him has been growing. Then she learns a terrifying secret about Tal, that throws her into emotional turmoil and she draws away from him.

Now…

Sonny learns about Tal's past demons and that draws the two of them closer together. As the oppressive bonds of pain begin to loosen, and she starts to think she might become whole again, she runs into someone from her past, and that encounter strips her of all the progress she's gained.

Tal wants to kill the man who hurt Sonny so horrendously and his actions bring out his violent nature, shocking him and Sonny. As a result, Tal raises a barrier between them that might be too devastating for either of them to get past.

Will Tal walk away, denying the future they could have together? Or will Sonny be able to convince him that, despite what they've both suffered, love can conquer all?

This volume includes:
#3: Dirty Talk, Sweet Release
#4: Dirty Talk, Blissful Surrender

Erotic Audios

In this series, Sonny listens to erotic audios that Tal makes for her. If you'd like to buy them for yourself, go to **OpalCarew.com/DirtyTalk**

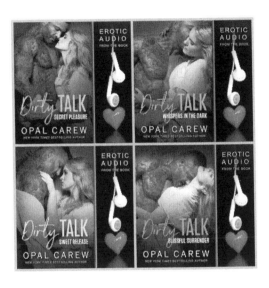

DIRTY TALK, BOOKS 3 & 4

OPAL CAREW

DIRTY TALK, SWEET RELEASE

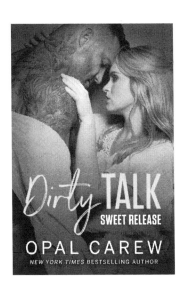

From the end of Dirty Talk, Whispers in the Dark

Sonny's phone rang and she glanced at the display. It was Leandra.

"Hi," Sonny said.

"Hey, there. I wanted to let you know that it looks like you were right to avoid that guy your friend introduced you to at the party."

"You mean Tal? Why?"

"I've just sent you an email. Check it out."

Sonny glanced at her screen and saw Leandra's message appear. She opened it. All that was inside was a link.

"What is this?"

"Just click on it."

Sonny moved the cursor over the link and clicked. A new tab opened with an image of a man with extensive tattoos on his arms. Not as dense as Tal's were, but her eyes jerked to his face and it was definitely Tal.

Her stomach clenched.

Tal was in handcuffs, escorted by a uniformed policeman. It was the front page of a newspaper.

Her gaze lurched to the headline.

Man Murders Father.

Tal heard an apartment door open and close and he

walked to the peephole to peer out, pretty sure it was Sonny's door.

All night, he couldn't stop thinking about the small sounds she'd made when she'd been snuggled under that blanket on her couch listening to him talk to her. Fuck, it was the hottest thing he'd ever experienced.

Her whimpers… and, fuck, seeing the movements under the blanket, that he'd known were her hands moving over her body as he'd described what he wanted her to do… and what he'd wanted to do *to* her… His cock swelled at the memory. And then her soft moans that had increased until she'd come right in front of him. How he'd been able to keep his cool and stay planted in that chair was a wonder.

Of course, knowing what had happened to her, he would never push her to go faster than she could handle. No matter how much patience it took. No matter how painful it became for him. His cock could complain all it wanted, he wouldn't do anything to frighten Sonny.

He heard footsteps in the hall, and sure enough, he saw Sonny pass by. He opened the door and stepped out.

"Sonny," he said, seeing her a few feet down the hallway walking toward the elevator. His gaze locked on the gentle sway of her delightful ass in her snug jeans.

She turned and gazed at him, her stance tentative.

"Oh, uh… hi." She pulled the bag that was slung over her shoulder closer to her body.

"I was going to come over and invite you out to lunch, then I heard your door open," he said. "What do you say?"

She frowned, her gaze shifting to the floor.

"I have some errands to run, then I have a lot of work to do today."

It was Saturday, but he knew she was self-employed, and sometimes had time crunches.

"Okay," he said, "but you still have to eat. We don't have to be out long. We could go right now if you like."

Her long, blonde hair shimmered in the light as she shook her head.

"No, I really can't."

He found it disconcerting that she wouldn't look at him. Clearly, she was embarrassed by what they'd done the other night. But it had been good for her. It had been a major step forward, her trusting him that much.

"Okay, then how about dinner?"

She shook her head nervously. "Today's not a good day."

He was determined not to let her slip back into her shell, shutting him out.

He tipped his head. "Sonny, I'm a patient man.

Just tell me when *is* good for you and we'll do it then."

"Um… I'm not sure."

He frowned. "Sonny," he said softly. "I can tell that you're a little uncomfortable with what we did the other night. Maybe a little embarrassed. I want us to talk about it. We made a good step forward, and I want us to keep making progress."

She sucked in a deep breath. "I just can't right now," she said, her voice sounding a bit shaky.

"Baby, I just want us to talk." He took a step forward and she jerked back.

His chest constricted. Fuck, right this instant, with her large brown eyes wide as a frightened deer's, she looked terrified. As if she actually thought he might hurt her.

Damn, he had to put that out of his mind. Believing she feared he would harm her. He'd just seen that look in so many women's eyes that he assumed it every time. Had already assumed it about Sonny.

But Sonny had reason to be nervous around any man, not just him, and sometimes, especially if he startled her, she was going to look at him like this. As much as it hurt, he knew she was reacting to her gut and he couldn't blame her for that.

He just had to remind himself of the immeasurable trust she had shown him. That had gone a long way to healing his own scars, as well as hers.

"Okay," he said in as calm a voice as he could muster. "Maybe tomorrow."

She drew in a deep breath and nodded. "I… really have to go now."

She turned and hurried down the hall. He watched as she stopped in front of the elevator halfway down the hall and pushed the button.

It wasn't going to be an easy path with her. But everything in him knew it would be worth it. To help her.

Helping her back across the threshold of fear would probably be one of the most important things he could ever do in his life.

It might even help him feel whole again.

Sonny's heart pounded as she waited for the elevator to arrive. Tal still stood at his door watching her.

Finally, the doors whooshed open and she escaped inside. She leaned against the elevator wall and sucked in a breath.

When she'd left her apartment and started down the hall on her way to pick up some groceries, she'd heard a door unlatch. She'd prayed it not be Tal, but her request had been denied. As she'd hurried past his door, he'd stepped into the hall behind her.

So many feelings had swirled through her at that moment.

Her mind had immediately returned to the memory of her lying on her couch yesterday, him on the chair across from her.

And his deep, sexy voice.

She still couldn't believe she'd done such intimate things in front of him. Even though she was hidden under a blanket, he knew what she was doing. He'd seen her face, the movement of the blanket as she'd stroked herself.

And he'd heard her intimate sounds as she'd come.

She covered her face with her hands, sucking in air to calm herself.

Everything he'd said in the hallway just now, though, had been so caring. His voice filled with concern. He wanted to help her. She believed that.

But she couldn't forget the newspaper image of him handcuffed and being taken to jail.

The elevator doors opened and she stepped into the sunlit lobby and walked to the entrance. She opened the glass door and stepped into the beautiful sunny day, gazing at the clear blue sky as she breathed in the sweet scent of the colorful flowers.

She was confused and uncertain. She didn't want to give up what she'd started with Tal, but the article had talked about his background, with gang associations, brutal behavior, and several calls to the police by neighbors about domestic violence involving his father and a younger brother. The whole thing painted a grim picture of who Tal was.

But it also contradicted everything she sensed about him.

The deep calmness she felt when she heard his tender, caring voice told her he was not that kind of man.

She had no idea how to reconcile the two conflicting views.

And making the wrong choice could have terrifying results.

Tal placed the sandwich into a container and tossed it into the bag with a bottle of water and an apple and headed to the door.

Since he wouldn't be having lunch with Sonny, he decided he'd go for a walk to clear his head, then eat by the water. Steve often went down to Hog's Back Park to have lunch by the falls, or even further down the river, depending on his mood. Maybe he'd be there and they could talk. Tal could use some friendly advice, though he'd have to be careful what he said. He would never betray Sonny's trust.

He went down the elevator and stepped out into the warm, sunny day. He walked along the sidewalk, over the bridge, then turned into the park. There were several people standing at the lookouts viewing the falls, but he didn't see Steve. He continued walking, enjoying the view of the glistening water and the abundant greenery around him, then followed a path leading into the shade of thicker trees. There were several people enjoying the park. Walking dogs, playing Frisbee, and eating picnic lunches.

After a few minutes, he spotted Steve sitting at a table talking with a woman. As he got closer, he realized the woman was Leandra, Sonny's friend. After the party, she and Steve had hooked up and were now seeing each other.

They seemed to be engrossed in their conversation and hadn't noticed him approaching yet. As he got closer, he could hear Leandra's voice.

"How well do you know this guy Tal?" Leandra asked.

Steve set down his sandwich and took a sip of his pop.

"We've known each other since university. He's basically my best friend."

She leaned forward. "Did you know that…" She frowned and stared at her water bottle. "That he was arrested for murdering his father?"

Tal stopped cold, shock jolting through him. Hell, this was bad news.

"Where did you hear that?" Steve demanded.

"It was a newspaper article I found on-line. It showed him being arrested. The article mentioned that he was involved with a gang and that the police had been called to his home numerous times for violent episodes."

Steve knew the whole story. When they'd gotten close in university, Tal had told him all of it in confidence. Tal knew Steve wouldn't betray that trust by telling Leandra, or anyone else, anything about it.

Steve shook his head. "All I can say is, I've know Tal for a long time and he's a great guy. I'd trust him with my life."

"Well, it seems like that wouldn't be such a great idea. And I'm really worried about the fact that he's interested in Sonny."

Steve's gaze jerked to hers. "You can't tell Sonny about this. I don't know what demons she's dealing with, but you don't want her to think she's living next door to a killer. And more importantly, no matter what you think, I believe Tal is good for her."

Leandra frowned. "It's too late. I already sent her the article."

Tal's chest constricted and his fists clamped into balls.

Ah, fuck. *That's* why Sonny reacted the way she did this morning. Like a deer facing a wolf.

"Why the hell did you do that?" Steve demanded.

"Because she's my friend and I want to protect her."

Steve shook his head.

"I don't know how you can be so convinced the guy won't hurt her," she said. "If you know something about it… if there's something I'm missing… then explain it to me."

Tal strode forward. "Don't you think it's me you should be asking?"

Leandra's head jerked around and her eyes widened.

Then he saw it. The fear.

She sucked in a deep breath and seemed to cringe.

He stood at the end of the rough-hewn wooden table, glaring at her.

But to her credit, she sucked in a deep breath and pushed back her shoulders.

"Was the article true?" she asked evenly.

"Not exactly," he said, his voice dead calm. "It wasn't my father. It was my stepfather."

Then he turned and strode away.

Sonny stared at her phone, the text Leandra had just sent her slowly sinking in.

Just saw Tal in the park. He admitted it! He murdered his stepfather!

Oh, God. She had hoped there was some explanation. That the whole thing was a lie, or that he'd been framed.

But he'd admitted the crime to Leandra.

A knock sounded on her door and she walked to the entrance and peered out.

Her heart thudded when she saw Tal on the other side of the door.

She opened the door, the chain still on.

"Hello," she said, keeping her voice even.

"Your friend sent you an article about me," he said bluntly.

She sucked in a breath. "Yes."

"So where does that leave us?"

It was all too much to handle. She shook her head.

"I don't know."

"Fuck," he mumbled. Then he tugged something from his pocket and handed it to her. It was a flash drive. "Here. I recorded this for you."

She took it from him. The brush of his large fingers against hers sent electricity quivering through her.

"What is it?"

"It's an audio I made for you. I used my cell to record what I said to you the other night and I made this audio from it."

"You recorded us?" The thought of him listening to that recording… hearing the sounds she'd made when she came… made her cheeks flame.

He frowned. "Don't worry. I'm not going to post it on the Internet or anything. I knew at the time I wanted to make this audio to help you, so you could listen to it any time."

It was hard to breathe with all the conflicting emotions tumbling through her.

"Thank you," she said quietly, the words carried on a breath of air.

His hard gaze locked on her and she felt her body start to tremble.

"Will you let me in so we can talk about it?" he asked evenly.

Panic surged through her as images flashed through her mind. Of him in handcuffs. Of words from the newspaper article, as if jumping off the page. *Gang member. Violent tendencies. Arrested several times. Gruesome scene. His father's bloody, battered body.*

She realized her head was shaking back and forth.

His mouth formed a thin line.

"Fuck it!" He turned and started to walk away.

She stood frozen at the door, the drive in her trembling hand, not sure what to do.

The fact that he'd killed someone, especially

someone close to him, and that he had a violent nature, confused and frightened her. She'd suffered at the hands of a violent man and his friends. Those men had had a veneer of respectability, but under the surface, they were ruthless and cruel.

On the other hand, with Tal she felt safe and protected. She couldn't believe he was the brutal man depicted in that article.

Sonny was terrified to let him in. Terrified he might hurt her. But as the storm of conflicting emotions swirled around her, she realized that she was even more terrified of losing him.

But she needed time.

She squeezed her hand around the cold flash drive he'd given her. Small and black. Containing the words he'd spoken to her yesterday. The words that had opened a door for her that had been closed tight for so long.

And she realized, time is exactly what he'd given her all along. He hadn't pushed her, even when he'd clearly been suffering with need because his body was hard for her. He'd been patient and kind. Loving and tender.

No matter what some stranger in an article said about him… no matter what some picture alluded to…none of it changed the man he was. What she heard in his voice. What she felt when she was with him. And the compassionate way he treated her.

She pushed the door closed and slid the chain off then opened it and burst into the hall.

"Tal, wait!"

But his apartment door was already open and he was going inside.

"Please!"

He glanced at her, his eyes cold and hard.

Then a flash of fur grabbed her attention and she realized that Mia had just streaked out the door and was racing down the hall at full speed.

"Oh, God! Mia."

If she got into the elevator, or the stairwell, she'd be frightened. She might even get outside. Sonny's heart crumpled at the thought of losing her.

Mia was already halfway down the hallway.

Tal stepped back into the hallway but before either of them could start running after the furry creature, the sound of an apartment door opening far down the hall, then voices, had Mia stopping dead in her tracks.

As the voices came closer, Mia, clearly frightened, turned tail and raced back up the hall, but instead of running to Sonny's apartment, she headed straight to Tal and leaped onto his denim-clad leg and climbed it like a tree trunk. He grabbed her, and tucked her against his chest, snuggled in the crook of his muscular arm, and she cowered there, peering out from the protection of his body.

Tal turned to Sonny, his expression still drawn tight in anger. As he walked toward her with Mia safely in his arms, she sucked in a breath.

But as he got closer, she realized that what she'd thought was anger, was actually pain. His eyes glinted as he tried to hide it, but she could see it there.

Because she'd rejected him.

She wasn't used to having power over a man, in any way. The thought confused her. And in this case, saddened her.

She didn't want to hurt Tal. Ever.

When he reached her door, he tried to tug Mia from his body so he could hand her to Sonny, but Mia's claws were embedded in his shirt so tightly, he couldn't pull her away. He pulled free one tiny paw, but as he tried to free the next, she squirmed and the first paw connected with his shirt again.

Although Sonny could feel tears welling in her eyes from her tumultuous emotions, the sight of him trying to pull the determined cat from his shirt made her break out in nervous giggles.

His gaze shot to hers and she looked properly contrite.

"If you bring her inside, she'll probably let go," she offered.

His lips compressed in a straight line as he

followed her back to her door, then inside. She closed the door behind him, then turned to take the cat from him, but Mia leaped from his arms and scurried down the hall.

He turned and reached for the doorknob, but she stepped in front of him, blocking his path.

She rested her hand on his arm.

"Tal, please stay."

Tal drew in a deep breath, allowing the closeness of her, the feel of her delicate fingers on his arm, to calm him.

When she'd shut him out, not even giving him a chance to explain, his whole world had crumbled around him. Having Sonny accept him—and more, look to him for help—had meant more to him than he could ever conceive.

This past that hung over him… this awful shadow… threatened everything that mattered to him. Love. Family. Having one special person to share his life with, who cared about him as much as he cared about her.

He nodded and let her guide him to the couch where he sat down. She settled in beside him.

She took his hand, entwining her fingers with his.

"Tal, the things they said in that article…" She shook her head. "I don't believe them."

It would be so easy to just accept that. She was giving him a free pass to just put it all behind him and move forward.

But that would be a lie. And that was no foundation for any kind of relationship.

And it certainly wouldn't be fair to her after she'd opened up to him so completely.

He squeezed her hand gently.

"But I'm afraid it's the truth."

Sonny's heart pounded in her chest. She wasn't sure she wanted to hear what he had to say.

"My mother remarried when I was fourteen," he explained. "The guy convinced her he was a knight in shining armor, ready to take care of her and her two sons. She'd been alone and struggling since we lost my dad. She couldn't see what he really was. He had a nice house, a good job. She wanted to feel safe. But once they were married, he treated her like a slave. He bullied her and kept her isolated. If she went to visit a neighbor, he'd beat the crap out of her. If she didn't have dinner on the table when he walked in the door, he'd beat the crap out of her."

Sonny felt ill, remembering the beatings she'd suffered at the hands of… *him.*

"Fuck, Sonny, you're trembling. This must be bringing up bad memories for you."

She squeezed his hand. "It's okay. I want to hear it all."

He nodded. "I tried to step in… to protect her… but he was bigger than me and just sent me flying cross the room with one whack. But sometimes it distracted him enough that he'd leave mom alone."

Sonny's stomach clenched at the thought of younger Tal being beaten by his stepfather.

"By the time I was fifteen, I'd started hanging out with a tough crowd, learning to fight, getting into trouble. Then one day, I came home to find that he'd pushed her and she'd hit her head on the granite counter. She went into a coma. He told the police it was an accident and, of course, they believed him."

He sighed, staring off into space.

"She died a week later. If it had been just me, I would have taken off at that point, but I couldn't leave my younger brother alone with this guy. So I learned to act tougher. To look tougher. I was pretty small at fifteen, but over the next year I grew to over six feet tall. I made it clear that if he laid a finger on Joey, I'd break every bone in his body."

Sonny rested her hand on his arm, disturbed not only by his words and the harrowing past he'd had to endure, but also by the haunting sadness in his eyes.

"Finally, he couldn't handle it any longer. Being subdued by his teenaged stepson. One night, he got drunk and attacked me with a butcher knife. He caught me off guard, coming at me from behind, and got in a few slashes before I knocked him to the ground and wrestled the knife from him. Once I let him up, he lunged at me. When I stepped out of the way, he went flying through the front window and sliced his neck open on the glass. When the police showed up, they assumed I initiated the fight and killed him. Especially with my history."

Sonny's heart ached for him. "I'm so sorry, Tal."

He shook his head, then focused on her. "The charges didn't stick. But that doesn't change the fact that I wanted to kill that bastard every single day. And one day I probably would have."

Sonny shook her head. "I don't believe it. That's not the kind of man you are."

"Baby, have you taken a look at me lately? Everything about me is designed to intimidate."

"Because you wanted to protect the ones you loved, and that was the only way you had." She smiled. "And I love how you look. Strong and confident."

She ran her hand along his muscled forearm. "I feel safe with you."

~

Tal's heart swelled at Sonny's words. At her total acceptance.

He slid his arm around her and held her close. She snuggled against him.

"Baby, I don't ever want you to be afraid of me, for any reason."

She stroked his cheek, and tipped up her face, her brown eyes glowing. He couldn't resist. He dipped his head down and brushed his lips against hers. She slid her arms around his neck and pulled him in closer, deepening the kiss.

He swept his tongue into her mouth and stroked, enjoying the delight of her softness.

Then he felt something on his shoulder and a raspy sensation against his ear. He drew back and turned his head to see two green feline eyes staring at him. Mia, half on the couch back and half on his shoulder. She began licking his ear again.

Sonny began to laugh. "Mia, stop that."

He smiled. "Don't worry about it. She just wants a little love."

He wrapped his hands around the cat and held her to his chest. She snuggled against him, then stretched out on his arm and purred.

"You're there for a while now," Sonny said. "Once she gets comfy, she settles in for a good long nap." She smiled. "I could put on a movie if you like."

"Didn't you say you have a lot of work to do today?"

She bit her lip. "I lied. I finished the project this morning. I just wasn't ready to talk to you yet. I'm really sorry."

"It's okay. I get it." He smiled, stroking the small furry critter in his arms. "So that movie sounds great. And maybe some water?"

Sonny stood up and glanced through her Blu-ray library, then pulled out one she thought Tal would like and put it in the device. Then she went into the kitchen to grab a couple bottles of water. By the time she got back, Tal was asleep, Mia still curled up against him.

Sonny smiled and grabbed the blanket from the arm of the couch and laid it over him, draping it below where Mia lay sleeping. Not that it was cold, but she always found the light blanket to be comforting, and she wanted to give Tal that comfort, too. Especially after he'd opened up to her about his tragic past.

She sat down in the armchair across from the couch with her laptop, and watched him. Everything about him was big and masculine. His hulking body. His dense, bristly, almost black whiskers and thick hair shaved close to his scalp on the sides, longer on top. His huge feet propped up on the ottoman.

All that contrasted against the sight of his muscular arm, covered in tattoos, curled around Mia. Seeing the small ball of fur nestled against him… remembering the gentleness with which he'd stroked the little cat… made her heart topple.

He was so good at giving comfort, and love.

Her chest ached at everything he'd been through. He deserved better. He deserved to be loved. To be cherished and cared for.

She wished she could take him in her arms right now and hold him close. Prove to him that he was a very special, wonderful man.

Tal opened his eyes and blinked at the bright after-noon sunshine. He glanced toward the purring coming from his lap. There was a soft, fleecy blanket over him, and Mia, Sonny's audacious little cat, had moved from his chest to being curled up on his stomach.

"I told you she'd keep you there for a long nap."

He laughed and stretched his arms, then stroked Mia's soft fur.

Then he glanced at Sonny, sitting on the armchair across from him. The same armchair he'd sat on the other night when he'd talked her through an orgasm. And he was where she'd been, the same blanket around him, his feet on the same ottoman.

At the memory of her face as she'd come, heat stirred in his groin and spread through his body.

She had her laptop open and she wore ear buds. Her face and neck were flushed and his gaze jerked to the side of the computer to see the black flash drive he'd given her sticking out the side.

His eyebrow darted up.

"Are you listening to the recording I gave you?"

Her cheeks turned a deeper rose color.

"Yeah… Seeing you where I was the other night… and me being where you were… reminded me. So I listened."

A wide smile crept across his face.

"So you like it?"

She nodded, the rapid movement of her head and the eagerness in her eyes skyrocketing his ego.

The thought of her listening to the sexy audio while she watched him sleep… and wondering how turned on she was… had his cock swelling.

Mia's eyes popped open and she mewed, then stood up and leaped away. He couldn't blame her. His rising erection had changed the landscape of her cat bed.

"So would you like to come snuggle up beside me and listen to it together?" he suggested.

He loved the idea of touching her while she got

turned on by his voice, even it if was just to have his arm around her. To be close enough to hear her heartbeat start to race. To hear her soft breathing as she got excited.

"I'd like to. But there's something else I've been thinking about."

"Oh, yeah? And what's that?"

"In the recordings," she said, "you're watching the woman and… that's really exciting…"

He put his feet on the floor and sat up straighter, then tossed the blanket beside him.

"Okay. Would you rather I do something different? Maybe pretend I'm blindfolded? Or that we're on the phone?"

He was sure she was asking him for more distance. So she could hear his voice, but not feel that he was watching her, even on a recording. If that's what she wanted, he'd give it to her.

"No, that's not it. I just…"

She pulled the ear buds from her ears and bit her lip.

"What is it, Sonny? You can tell me."

"I'd like to… um… to watch you…"

He waited, but she just fidgeted, her cheeks blooming an even darker red.

Did she mean watching him as he talked? Or did she mean…his cock twitched… she wanted to watch him jack off?

He raised an eyebrow. "You want to watch me come?"

She bit her lip.

"Well… uh… I'd like to know that you're… I mean… I don't know if you did last time… And I'm not asking you to tell me, I just…

He fought back a grin. She was so adorable.

"I want to know what it's like," she continued, "to be in the same room with a man when… to feel safe with a man when…"

Sonny had seen the heat flare in his eyes when she'd told him she wanted to watch him, then amusement glitter as she'd backpedalled.

Now, his expression grew compassionate.

"I get it, baby. I'll do anything to help you. You know that."

She wrapped up her ear buds and put them in the little case she had for them so Mia wouldn't chew through the cord.

"So when would you like to do it?" he asked.

God, she was so turned on from listening to the recording he'd made for her … her nipples hard and tight… her vagina clenching in need… that she wanted to do it right now.

"When would *you* like to do it?" she asked.

"Baby, just the thought has me ready to go."

"Okay." She bit her lip. "Then… now?"

He chuckled. "Okay. Hold on. Come over here for a second."

He patted the couch beside him.

She closed her laptop and set it on the side table, then stood up and walked toward him, wondering what he was going to do. She sat beside him.

He slid his muscled arm around her waist and drew her near. He kissed the top of her head and she shivered in delight. He was so much bigger than her. She felt so tiny in comparison. Just like Mia had looked curled in the crook of his arm.

"I think you need a little time for this idea to sink in," he said. "Maybe we'll have dinner first, relax, and then we'll talk about exactly what you want."

"But I told you already."

"Yes, and that was great. I think you should get used to expressing what you want. And how you want it. You've shown an extraordinary level of trust in me, and that makes me feel really good. I want you to trust me. I also want you to be able to express yourself fully to me."

She gazed up at him with wide eyes.

"Don't worry, I'm not asking for crazy intimate details. Just enough so I know what to do without making you nervous." He smiled and kissed her forehead. "Not that we won't push some limits, since that's what you need right now. Okay?"

"Okay."

He took her hand and stood up, drawing her with him. "So why don't we go to my place and I'll make some dinner. Then we can decide if we want to stay there or come back here."

The thought of sitting in his apartment while they did this excited her. Being in his environment, where he slept, where he showered, where he gave himself pleasure… maybe while thinking about her.

She followed him out the door and back to his place. Stepping inside felt strange. Ordinarily the thought of being in a man's apartment, alone with him, would fill her with blind terror. But it was different with Tal.

He'd helped her take huge steps forward.

And the one she'd take with him after dinner had her pulse fluttering.

He led her to the couch. "Just sit down and I'll bring you a glass of wine, then get dinner started."

But when he tried to draw his hand away, she didn't want to let go.

"You don't have to go to any trouble. We could just order a pizza."

"It's no trouble." He smiled and kissed her hand. "Don't worry. It won't be long. I already made a pan of lasagna for tonight that I'll just put in the over then pull together a salad. So sit."

She sat down, their fingers sliding apart.

He walked into the kitchen and returned a few minutes later with a glass of red wine. He handed it to her and then turned on some music.

About ten minutes later, he returned with his own glass of wine and sat beside her.

"It'll be ready in about forty minutes. If you're really hungry, we could have the salad ahead of time."

She gazed up at him, and her eyes must have shown that food wasn't what she was hungry for, because his deep blue eyes heated. She ran her hand over his bristly cheek, growing weak with need at the masculine feel of him.

She tipped up her face in invitation. His arm slid around her and his face lowered. Anticipation built in her as his lips drew nearer, then when they brushed hers, she felt faint.

As the pressure of his mouth increased, she slid her arms around his neck, pulling him in closer. Her heart raced as his tongue glided over her lips and she opened, welcoming him inside. The gentle sweep of his tongue made her feel treasured.

She was lost in the gentle strokes of his tongue, the tenderness of his mouth moving on hers. She felt totally enveloped in his presence.

Protected. Cared for.

Wanted.

Their lips parted and she gazed into his eyes, seeing the reflection of her own need for a deep connection with someone.

She stroked his raspy cheek. "I love it when we kiss."

He smiled. "So do I."

"It's so intimate. So sweet. It makes me feel special."

His blue eyes gleamed with loving sincerity.

"You are special, sweetheart."

He stroked her hair behind her ear, sending tingles down her neck.

"I know with what happened to you," he said, "it's hard for you to trust a man. I'm glad you trust me enough to open up like this."

She drew him back to her and found his lips again. His arms slid around her in a full embrace and he pulled her tighter to him, his tongue delving deeper this time. She suckled on it, wishing he could be nestled inside her forever.

His hand slid under her hair, then his fingers glided up the back of her head, threading through the strands. The kiss became more passionate. She melted against him, her heart thumping in her chest. The feel of his hard body against her, his thick arms around her, made her weak with desire.

"If we keep this up, I'm going to have trouble

stopping," he murmured against her lips, then took them again.

She pressed her tongue into his mouth and swirled deep.

He drew back, even though she clung to him.

"Okay, sweetheart. I know you're not ready for where this is taking us."

He drew her hands from around his neck and entwined his fingers with hers, then kissed the back of her hand. He picked up her glass of wine and handed it to her. She sipped, watching him over the rim of the glass, a warm quivering feeling inside at how protective he was of her.

"I'm going to bring out the salad now."

They sat down at the table and enjoyed the Caesar salad together, then he brought out the lasagna. He put a portion on her plate, and she took a bite.

"Mmm. This is delicious," she said. "You're a great cook."

"Thank you."

He refilled her wine glass and she took a sip. She felt so relaxed. Being here in his apartment. Enjoying his company. Just like they were on a date.

He was right. She had made huge strides forward.

Because of him.

She swirled the wine in her glass as she watched him.

He had his own baggage. His early years had been tragic. Losing his father. Doing his best to protect his mother and little brother at such a young age. Then her death, leaving him alone to look out for his sibling. He'd had to grow up so fast and become so tough.

"Thank you for telling me about your past," she said softly. "It must have been difficult to dredge it all up again."

"I've never told anyone about it before, except for Steve."

He took another bite of his food, and she thought he was going to close up, but then he turned his gaze to her.

"But I'm glad I shared it with you."

Her heart swelled and she rested her hand on his. He lifted it and kissed her fingers. The gentle touch sent delightful shimmers of heat through her.

"I don't want to pry, but do you mind if we talk about it some more?"

She thought it would help him to share his story, and she really wanted to know more about what had happened and how he had coped.

"Sure. Ask whatever you want."

"Okay. So what happened after your stepfather died?"

"They arrested me, as you saw in the article. It

OPAL CAREW

looked pretty bad for a while. The police saw me as some thug involved with gangs, prone to violence, and figured it was an open and shut case. But then they looked into his background and uncovered past complaints against him from a previous marriage. That pieced together with hospital records showing his dead wife and current step-sons having had suspicious injuries, gave credi-bility to my account of what happened that night."

Her heart ached.

His dead wife and current stepsons.

He meant himself.

"So they let you go." She was so glad he hadn't been put in prison.

"Once they realized I was the victim, yeah."

"And your brother… It sounds like you were able to protect him from being physically harmed by your stepfather."

"Mostly."

The haunted look in his eyes told her he'd had to witness at least one time when his younger brother had been hurt. She squeezed his hand.

"So what happened to Joey and you afterward?"

"Joey was only thirteen and they wouldn't let me be his guardian since I was too young. If the two of us went into foster care together, I knew that I'd be hurting his chances of being taken into a good home. And I sure as hell wasn't going to abandon him to the system. I knew that our real dad had a brother in the UK and when the authorities contacted him, he and his wife were willing to take us in."

"That's great. But you didn't go with him?" Hadn't they wanted him?

"I did go with him at first. Stayed with them for about six months, but then came back here. Joey was happy there. They had a daughter about my age and a son who was a year younger than Joey. They became friends really fast and I saw that Joey loved being the big brother for a change."

"So why did you leave? I think there's more than you wanting Joey not to be eclipsed by you with your younger cousin."

He sighed. "Yeah, well as you've seen, I'm pretty sensitive about women being afraid of me. You can imagine how I felt when I saw dread in their daughter's eyes every time she looked at me. I'm sure she was convinced that I was going to drag her into a room and rape her the first chance I got. And it wasn't just her. Even my aunt looked at me with fear."

"You're such a wonderful man. That is so unfair."

He shrugged. "I can't blame them. I looked like an intimidating bad-ass. But even though I wasn't what they expected when they agreed to take in their two nephews who'd been abused by their stepfather, they really tried to make me feel welcome. I knew it was better for everyone if I dropped out of the picture. So I came back here and I was able to finish school and get student loans to put myself through university."

"That's great that you were able to turn things around for yourself. So what you do for a living?"

"I have a Masters in Sociology and currently I'm working on a study for the government of the effects on society of self-driving cars. I love the freedom of working from home and deciding my own hours."

"And you don't have to worry about co-workers perceptions of you. I understand all about that. Except that I stay away from other people because *I'm* afraid. You stay away because they're afraid of you."

She stroked his arm. "I'm sorry life has been so difficult to you."

He gazed at her and tightened his hand around hers.

"It hasn't treated you so well, either."

She smiled. "Until now."

"God, Sonny. Come here."

She stood up and he pulled her onto his lap, then cupped her face and kissed her with a tenderness that melted her heart. One hand glided down her back while the other curled around her head, drawing her close to his body, her breasts crushed against his solid chest, her mouth meshed tight with his.

When he released her, she could barely catch her breath.

"I think I'm all done dinner," she said in a husky voice.

"Really?" He tucked his finger under her chin and tipped up her face, a devilish grin playing across his lips. "So does that mean you're ready for desert?"

Oh, God, she was so ready.

She nodded.

"Good. I have ice cream. And I think there's some leftover blueberry pie."

Her jaw dropped and he just laughed.

"I take it that's not what you had in mind."

He kissed her again. Brief but intense. Then he lifted her to her feet as he stood up. Now their bodies were tight together, their gazes locked.

"I think we should finish our wine in the living room," he suggested.

She just nodded.

He picked up her wine glass and pressed his hand to the small of her back, then guided her to the living room.

"I think you'll be comfortable here," he said as he gestured to an armchair.

He handed her the glass, then cleared away the

dishes, returning a few moments later with his own glass and sat on the couch facing her.

"You made a request earlier," he said, settling back. "I think it's time."

She shifted in her chair. "Yes. That would be… good."

He leaned forward, his elbows resting on his knees. "Now, sweetheart, I want you to be completely open and honest with me right now. I don't want you to be embarrassed by what you like. Or what turns you on. And I don't want to go too fast for you, so if you don't tell me, I'll play it cautious."

She drew in a deep breath.

"I want you to talk," she said slowly. "Like in the audios. Tell me what you're thinking about. What you like. I want this to be totally about you and your pleasure."

His eyes twinkled. "Well, not totally. Because the idea of me coming turns you on, right?"

She bit her lip. "Yes. But it's not just about… um… coming. You've done so much for me. And part of that is helping me understand what excites me. I want to know what excites you."

He smiled. "Okay. What else?"

She gazed at him, and the open acceptance in his eyes calmed her.

"I want to hear you. Having that pleasure. To

see you." She felt her cheeks flame. "I mean… your face."

He laughed. "My face. Okay."

He sipped his wine, pondering.

"So, is it really just my face you want to see? Because if so, I'll grab a blanket and keep my cock hidden. Because, baby, it's going to come out of my jeans at some point."

Her gaze fell to his crotch, and seeing the fabric stretched over his already growing bulge sent heat simmering through her.

"I…" She sucked in a breath. She desperately wanted to see his big, male member. "I don't want you to hide it."

He chuckled. "Okay, I think we're ready to go."

He stood up and drew the drapes, closing off the sight of the setting sun, then turned on a small lamp. The room was cast in a soft light. Dim enough so it was relaxing, but lit well enough so she could see him—and his body—clearly.

He sat back down and pulled his cell from his pocket and tapped on it a couple of times, then set it down.

Was he recording this to make another audio for her later? So she could listen again and again? Her body quivered at the thought.

He leaned back and drew in a deep breath. Then his gaze drifted from her face down her body. Her skin heated and little bursts of excitement danced along her nerve endings at his acute male attention.

He took a few more deep breaths, then sighed deeply.

Hello, baby. I'm glad you're here with me again. I'm going to share one of my most intimate moments with you.

I'm going to take my time. Ramp it up nice and slow so you can really enjoy it.

Are you ready?

His gaze was on her and she nodded. The wide, satisfied smile that spread across his face took her breath away.

Good, baby. Because so am I.

She watched as his hand stroked over the front of his jeans. She sucked in a breath, wishing she was feeling what his fingers were feeling.

Right now, I'm sitting here fully dressed, but I've been thinking about you for hours and my cock is so hard… so big… it's painful inside these jeans. But before I do anything about that, I'm going to take off my shirt.

He grabbed the hem of his white T-shirt and pulled it over his head, then tossed it to the floor. His glorious muscles and dense tattoos were a sensational sight.

Now I'm sitting here in just my jeans, stroking my cock. I told you it's already rock hard and aching. I'm imagining you sitting in front of me, curled up in the big armchair, watching me. I can see the hunger in your eyes.

His gaze washed over her and she shivered.

I love that you want to watch me. To hear me.

I know the thought of me stroking my cock in front of you is turning you on. You want to see it. My hard cock. Throbbing in my hand as I stroke it.

Do you want me to show it to you, baby? Yeah?

She bit her lip, her eyes wide. She did. So badly. She didn't say so, but he smiled, reading it in her eyes.

Mmm, it's exciting knowing how much you want to watch me stroke myself.

Mmm. Yeah. In my imagination, you start to undo

43

*your top… a smile on your face… teasing me as you
slowly release one button at a time.*

Her fingers dropped to her top, resting on that
first button. She wanted to undo it. She wanted to
be the woman in his fantasy.

His gaze burned through her as she toyed with
the button, not meaning to tease him. Just aching to
be brave enough to take this step.

*I'm unzipping my jeans now, thinking about that.
Mmm. Thinking about seeing your beautiful breasts.*

He pulled the zipper down as he spoke and she
held her breath.

*I slide my fingers over my cock, still inside my jeans,
knowing you want to see it.*

Oh, God, she did. So badly.

His fingers slid inside and the sight of them
moving under fabric… knowing he was touching
his hard shaft… took her breath away.

*I think about your fingers unfastening your buttons
… your top falling open.*

She licked her lips and found herself undoing
the button on her top. His eyes heated and she

undid the second, then the third, watching his hand moving under the denim.

She sucked in a breath and released more buttons, letting her top fall open.

Oh, yeah, baby.

The heat in his voice singed her senses.

I squeeze my cock tightly. It's hard and ready. I can see the craving in your eyes.

She waited, her breath held, watching his hand.

You want to see what you're doing to me?

I will show you, baby. I promise. But first, I want you to open your top and let me see you.

She let the top slide from her shoulders a little, opening the front a little more so he could see her.

That's right, baby. Open it all the way.

Oh, God help her, she couldn't resist his words. She opened her top and let it slide off her shoulders and fall to the floor.

His eyes widened, then he laughed softly.

Oh, yeah. Just like that.

He hadn't expected that. But clearly he would encourage her. Trying to help her push past her boundaries.

Ah, fuck, I love the sight of your beautiful breasts all covered in that sweet baby blue lace bra.

Now I'm going to give you what you want. I'm pulling out my cock.

Her breath caught at the sight of his thick, stiff cock as he drew it into view. Oh, God, it was every bit as big as she'd imagined.

It was swollen and red, veins throbbing along the side. The head was as large as a plum.

His hand glided from the base to the tip, then down again.

She sucked in a breath at the sight.

He chuckled.

You like that, baby? Seeing my cock? Watching me stroke it?

She nodded, a deep ache building inside her as she watched his big hand, tightly gripping his cock, gliding up and down.

Now you can watch my cock get harder as you show me more of your body.

I'm pumping it for you. Knowing how much you love watching me do it… is pushing me closer to the edge.

He stroked his cock slowly. The tip disappearing and reappearing in the embrace of his hand. She longed to walk over to him and wrap her own hand around it. To feel it pulsing within her grip.

Oh, it feels so good. My cock is hard. I'm getting to that state where I'm close… and I'll stay there for a long time.

For you.

Ahh, fuck, baby, I want to see your naked breasts so badly. Take off your bra for me.

She wanted to give him what he wanted. He was giving her so much. As she reached behind herself to unhook her bra, his breath caught.

That's right. Show me your hard, aching nipples.

She dropped the straps, then slowly lowered her bra, revealing her naked breasts. A shiver rushed through her. No man had seen her naked since…

She pushed the thought from her mind and basked in the glow of his appreciative gaze. Oh, God, this is what it should feel like. Just like this.

She wanted him to look at her. To see how much he turned her on. She brushed her fingers over her hard nipples and he groaned.

Oh, fuck, baby, I love seeing you touch them. I love watching them get harder as your fingertips brush over them.

I'm stroking faster now. Pumping up and down.

Can you see my cock getting harder? Just for you.

She squeezed her nipples between her finger-tips, her gaze glued to his enormous, swollen cock as his hand moved up and down the thick shaft.

Goddamn, you have me so fucking hot.

Oh, that's right baby, squeeze those nipples. Let me see them swell.

She watched his hand move up and down. His cock thick. The tip glistening with precum. Oh, God, was he really that hard because of her?

She was thrilled that the sight of his hard cock didn't frighten her. He wanted her and she wasn't afraid.

She *wanted* him to want her. To *see* her.

She cupped her breasts, squeezing them, then stroking her hard nubs again.

Ah, fuck, baby, that's so sexy. You touching your breasts like that.

Pinch those hard nipples for me, baby… as I stroke my cock for you.

She did as he asked, pinching them between her fingertips, feeling the ache spike through her body, straight to her pussy. Moaning at the quivering sensations pulsing through her.

Oh, fuck, baby, I want to see so much more of you. I want to see you naked. Want to see every part of your beautiful body.

Ohhh, yeah. Just the thought is making me harder. Taking me closer.

She bit her lip. She wanted to give him what he wanted. She wanted to be naked in front of him. To see his eyes as he looked at her. To see his cock swell even more.

She sucked in a breath, then ran her fingers over the button of her jeans.

Oh, God, baby. Fuck, yeah. Show me.

She unzipped her jeans, watching his eyes darken, turning her blood to liquid fire. His gaze glided down her newly exposed flesh, over her stomach to the top of her lacy blue panties, his soft groans and sounds of approval encouraging her.

Yeah, take off your jeans.

She stood up and pushed her jeans down. Goose bumps danced over her body, prickling across her skin. She flushed hotly, embarrassed at being half naked in front of him now, wearing only her panties, but his deep, needy breaths and the hot masculine appreciation in his eyes held her mesmerized.

Mmm, baby. Those tiny panties are so sweet, but there's a sweeter sight beneath them.

He pumped in a steady rhythm now, need glazing his eyes.

I… want… to… see… you.

He groaned softly.

All of you.

Oh, God, his need rippled through her and she couldn't help herself. She had to give him what he wanted. She needed to… because she desperately wanted it herself. To bare herself to him completely.

She tucked her fingers under the elastic.

Oh, fuck, baby. Yeah. Take them off. Show me your sweet pussy.

Quickly, before she could change her mind, she pushed down her panties.

Ohhh, baby. Oh, yeah. I'm so fucking turned on seeing you like that. I'm stroking my cock… pumping it harder…

She sat down, watching fascinated as his hand glided up and down, the head of his cock disappearing into his fist, them popping up again. She licked her lips, wishing she could lick the tip of him. Taste that glistening precum.

I see you watching my hand. The hunger in your eyes.

I love the sight of you completely naked in the chair. Sitting there waiting for me to come. Anticipating it.

You want to watch me pump my cock until I come? Imagine it pushing inside your aching pussy and riding it until you come right along with me?

Oh, God, the thought of his big cock pushing inside her… filling her full… made her tremble with intense desire.

Oh, baby, I can imagine my cock sliding into you. Ahh, fuck. Feeling your hot pussy gripping me tightly. The velvety softness of you around me.

Fuck, I'm so fucking close. I could come right now.

You want to see that, baby? See my cock explode in my hand, because of you? The cum pulsing out of me?

Her gaze was glued to his big, hard erection. Waiting… Wanting so desperately to see that.

God, I want to come so fucking badly.

Baby, open your legs for me. Slowly. As I pump my cock. Let me see that sweet pussy of yours.

She opened her legs, exposing her most intimate

flesh. The intense heat in his eyes washed through her, pushing her need higher.

She glided her hand down her stomach, then over her exposed folds.

His eyes widened, the pupils turning to a deep midnight blue.

Fuck, that's right. Stroke your pussy for me.

Oh, fuck. Is it wet, baby? Are you wet for me? Are you getting turned on watching me pump my cock for you?

"Yeah," she whimpered softly, barely able to catch her breath.

You have me so turned on it's going to feel incredible when I finally come.

I'm stroking my throbbing cock in my fist. Thinking about what it would be like to sink deep into your beautiful, swollen pussy. To feel how wet and hot it is around me.

He let out a long groan, his eyes filled with need.

Oh, yeah, baby. That would be so sweet.

I can barely hold on.

The sound of his trembling voice… knowing she affected him so intensely… thrilled her.

But I want you to come, too. Are you close, baby? Are you going to come for me?

She stroked her slick flesh faster. Pleasure pulsing through her. Swelling deep inside her and expanding outward.

"Oh, yes," she whimpered, sounding close to tears. She pushed her fingers into her wet opening, feeling the slick warmth inside. Thrusting them in and out.

Goddamn, you're so fucking sexy. God, keep finger fucking yourself like that. Ah, fuck, baby.

His deep groans and heavy breathing sent her whirling close to the edge.

Oh, yeah. Fuck. Stroke your clit for me.

She vibrated her fingertip over the little button, letting out a soft moan at the pleasure of it.

Oh, fuck, I don't think I can hold back. I'm going to fucking come any minute.

"Oh, please," she cried. "Yes. I want you to."

You want me to stroke faster for you, baby? Do you?

"Yes," she cried. "Oh, God, yes."

She watched his hand pump faster, and she stroked herself faster, too, matching his speed. Oh, God, it felt so good.

And she liked him watching her. She thought it would be different. Scary. But the desire in his eyes... the need... made her feel special. Wanted.

Oh, fuck... Oh, yeah.

I'm going to come for you, baby. I'm... ah, fuck... yeah.

The sight of his face, filled with such need... his long, breathy words... filled her with a desperate longing.

I'm... so... fucking... close.

Ah, fuck. Ah, fuck. Ahhhh, fuuuuuck!

She pumped her finger faster in her pussy, his raspy, masculine moans ramping up her pleasure to a fever pitch.

"Oh, God," she cried, then moaned long and loud as an orgasm washed over her.

Oh, yeah, baby. That's right. Oh, fuck, baby. Come for me.

You're so beautiful. I love… watching you… come. Knowing… I brought you… that pleasure.

His groans of pleasure and heavy, broken breathing, pushed her pleasure higher.

His hand still moved on his cock as he watched her, his eyelids half closed. A gleam in his eyes that took her breath away.

She soared higher, gliding on a cloud of ecstasy, as her whole body vibrated in pure bliss.

Oh, yeah. I'm fucking… coming… Oh, God… Ohhhh.

His groans of release filled her with euphoria. She watched him erupt, a white plume shooting into the air.

He drew in slow, deep breaths now.

Oh, yeah, baby. Mmm. That was so good. It felt fucking incredible.

Because of you, baby.

Thank you, baby.

Her moan slowly faded in her throat as she slumped back. Her legs were straight out in front of her and her head flopped on the cushioned back of the chair.

She was still dragging in deep breaths, floating on the afterglow of the spectacular orgasm, when she realized she was slumped on the chair, totally naked.

She pulled her hand away from her slick opening to her stomach, embarrassed that he'd seen her touching herself there, then immediately slid it back to cover herself, her cheeks burning. She slowly curled up like a furling leaf, trying to cover her naked breasts, too.

Tal watched Sonny as she withdrew into herself. The open, relaxed sexual being she'd been only seconds ago, withered into an embarrassed, vulnerable woman.

He drew in a deep breath as he slid away his cock and zipped up.

He had been shocked and delighted at the way she had responded to his words. The way she had watched him with intense hunger in her eyes. It had turned him on more than he had ever been in his life. Watching her open up and expose herself to him. Physically. And emotionally.

She had trusted him.

She had *wanted* him.

His cock twitched at the thought.

But now she needed him in a different way.

He picked up his t-shirt from the floor and stood up. He lifted the shirt in two hands, shaking it so it hung flat, keeping his gaze on it rather than her beautiful, naked body on the chair, her shimmering blonde hair mussed and trailing over her shoulders.

He laid it over her like a blanket and her fingers curled around the fabric, pulling it closer around her.

"Go ahead and put that on," he said softly, then turned around.

He could hear her moving and the rustle of the fabric as she pulled it on.

"Okay," she said softly.

He turned around. A smile turned up his lips at the sight of her. His t-shirt draped over her small frame like a tent. A smile that faded as he realized how it clung to her body, showing the outline of her breasts, her nipples still hard and pushing at the thin fabric.

He knelt in front of her. Her cheeks were crimson red and she wouldn't meet his gaze.

"Sonny, I want you to look at me, sweetheart."

Her brown-eyed gaze flickered to his, then away again. Her cheeks darkened in color.

He tucked his fingers under her chin and lifted, and this time their gazes collided, then locked.

"I don't want you to withdraw, or be embarrassed by what we did. You took a big step forward today. You should be proud of that." He ran his fingertips tenderly over her soft cheek. "You knew what you wanted, and you allowed yourself to have it."

Her eyes gleamed with some deep, unsettling emotion. She had so many demons to deal with he could only imagine what she must be going through.

"What we just shared was a beautiful experience and I am so glad I was a part of it." He stroked her hair back from her face and smiled encouragingly. "I'll never forget it."

She trembled under his touch and he wanted to pull her into his arms and hold her close, but he wouldn't jeopardize the fragile progress they had made.

"I want you to know," he said gently, "that I'm here for you in any way you need me right now. Okay?"

She nodded and long, tentative seconds lingered between them as both their hearts thumped in synch.

Was she going to pull away? Withdraw from him even more?

She sucked in a long, slow breath. Then to his total astonishment, she surged against him, flinging her arms around his neck. As she rested her head against his shoulder, burrowing in as close as she could, he tightened his arms around her. Holding her. Loving her right here, in the safety of his embrace.

He stroked her hair.

"Thank you, Tal."

Her soft words, spoken against his chest, were barely audible. But they seeped into him and sent his spirit soaring.

He tilted her chin up. "Thank you, baby."

Her sweet lips turned up in a small smile, then she lifted her head, parting her lips in invitation.

He dipped his head down, and brushed his lips against hers.

She murmured, then pulled him closer, deepening the kiss.

The pressure of her sweet mouth on his, the brush of her tongue against his lips, set his heart pounding.

He wanted her so much he could barely contain himself, but there was no way he'd make a move on her. Now or in the future. Not until she was totally ready.

He would protect her from anyone. And anything.

Even himself.

Their lips parted and she gazed up at him and smiled. She ran her hands from his neck down his shoulders. Then her gaze turned to his upper arm. Her fingers lovingly traced the long scar that cut through the ink work. Most people didn't notice it because of the density of his tattoos.

"What happened?" she asked.

"That's where my stepfather gashed me with the knife. There are two more." He pointed at the smaller scars on his arm.

She gazed at them, stroking her finger over them.

"I'm sorry you had such a difficult time," she said, compassion quivering in her voice. "You're such a wonderful man. You deserved so much better."

He smiled, then stroked her hair back, and cupped her sweet face between his hands.

Then he brushed his lips against hers in a sweet kiss.

"Well, it seems I've finally gotten what I deserve."

Sonny smiled as she gazed at the bright mix of purple, pink, and white petunias in the large barrel planter outside the restaurant where she and Tal were going to eat dinner. Tal had gone to park the car and she'd decided to wait outside rather than go in and get a table, since it was such a beautiful day outside.

Of course, everything seemed more beautiful to her ever since that wonderful, intimate experience between them [a few days ago]. She'd been awestruck by the whole thing, but especially the gentle way he'd drawn her back out when she'd started to fall prey to her old fears and withdrawn. With patience, and tender words, he'd ensured she didn't regress.

She noticed a sleek, back limousine pull up in front of the restaurant and stop, blocking traffic. The driver got out and opened the back door. A shiver raced through her as a man in a suit stepped out.

Any man in a suit, especially one with obvious wealth, set her heart twisting in fear, but she drew in a deep breath, willing herself not to fall into her old pattern. The man who had abused her, and his deplorable friends, were history. It happened years ago and far from here. She couldn't let them and what they did to her rule her life anymore. Especially now that she had met Tal, who was helping her get past the pain and regain control of her life.

Just seeing a rich man shouldn't send her into a tailspin.

So she drew her shoulders back and, instead of cowering as she stared at the ground waiting for him to disappear into the distance, she lifted her head high… and gazed in his direction.

Then froze.

Her hands began to tremble.

The man's steel gray eyes turned to her as he stepped onto the sidewalk, a flicker of recognition in their depths.

Then his lips turned up in a cold, feral smile. He waved away the man talking to him and stepped in her direction.

"I haven't seen you in long time," he said, his cold familiar voice dredging up a blue of horrific memories.

His gaze glided down her body and she felt as if she'd been stripped naked. She stood frozen in terror.

"I always thought you were one of D's best pets."

He was so close she could barely breathe. D had been how the other men had referred to the man who had kidnapped her. His friends whom he'd shared her with.

To her, he was just Master.

This man had been the worst of the lot. His sexual demands had been more degrading and abusive than even Master's. And he'd beaten her more viciously.

He reached out and stroked her cheek with one finger. She wanted to jerk back, but her body refused to move. When she'd been a prisoner, she'd been trained to stay still… allowing them to touch her as they wanted. The alternative had been severe beatings.

Or worse.

"It was a shame when he let you go. I could have enjoyed you for quite a bit longer."

The glint in his eye sent a chill through her.

He knew where she was. He could send someone to nab her anytime he wanted. And then she'd just disappear. Again.

She couldn't breathe. Her whole body trembled.

Then his cold, gray gaze flickered behind her and his arrogant confidence seemed to waver. Just a fraction.

That's when she realized Tal was behind her.

∾

Sonny & Tal's story continues in
Dirty Talk, Blissful Surrender
which follows.

DIRTY TALK, BLISSFUL SURRENDER

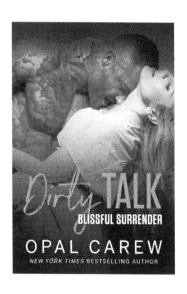

Tal parked the car, then walked along the sunny street a block down from the restaurant. This was officially their first date.

Sonny had come so far in a short while. After what they'd shared a week ago, where she'd actually bared herself to him, she'd been more relaxed around him.

They'd spent time together every day since then, and during that time she'd started casually touching him. Sometimes just a brush of her hand on his. Or she'd touch his cheek. She seemed to love it when his face was raspy with a dark shadow of whiskers.

And when they went to the pool and he took off his shirt, she would glide her fingertips lovingly over his scars, a wistful look in her doe eyes.

They were getting closer every day, and he knew that he wanted it to go on forever. They hadn't known each other very long, but he knew, deep in his heart, that she was the woman he was meant to be with.

He turned the corner onto the main street and walked toward the restaurant only a dozen yards ahead. Sonny was waiting for him by the decorative wrought iron fence surrounding the outdoor patio in front of the restaurant, near a large planter of flowers.

She was talking to a man in a suit. Tal was

behind her, but something about her stance… some aura he was picking up… sent his pulse surging. He picked up his pace and as he got closer, the guy looked up and saw him.

The arrogance in his eyes… with a cruel edge… put Tal on alert, every muscle ready to spring into action.

"Sonny, is everything all right?" he asked as he stepped beside her.

But he could see immediately that it was far from all right.

Her cheeks were flushed, her breathing shallow, and though she was looking at the man, not Tal, he could see the terror in her eyes.

"Sonny, who the hell is this?"

The monster standing in front of Sonny, who she had known as V, stared at her smugly, certain she wouldn't say anything. She knew that with their money, none of the men would ever be charged with what they'd done. They'd reminded her of that over and over again. It would be a 'he said, she said' situation and no one would take her word over these men of prestige.

And the thought returned to her that he could easily hire someone to find her and kidnap her. And there was nothing she could do about it.

"Sonny?" Tal's voice broke through her thoughts.

"He was one of them."

The words, in a shaky whisper, simply slipped from her mouth. She didn't mean for them to.

Tal's blue eyes flared like blazing fireballs and he surged forward. Tal's fist connected with V's jaw and he went down.

Her heart thundered as she watched Tal start pounding V in the face, beating him with his huge fists. She'd never seen such rage in a man's eyes and it terrified her.

Someone called 911 on their cell and a crowd formed around them, but no one seemed to quite know how to pull Tal off him.

Finally, she shook herself from her stupor and hurried forward.

"Tal, no. Please."

He didn't seem to hear her as his fist connected again.

"Tal. Stop this," she cried.

He hesitated, then lowered his fist. He stared at the man in front of him, whose face was bloody and broken, and let go of his grip on V's shirt. V slumped to the sidewalk.

Tal stood up and turned to Sonny. His eyes were haunted.

"Are you all right?" he asked.

Her gaze shifted to the splatter of blood on his face, to the smears of red on his fist.

She shook her head. Tears were streaming from her eyes. She wrapped her arms around herself, a chill running through her.

As he stepped toward her, concern washing across his face, she jerked back.

She didn't mean to. But memories of the beatings. Of the more intimate assaults, had reared up her terror of men.

This was Tal and she knew he wouldn't hurt her. But at the same time, this wasn't Tal. This was a side of him… an aggressive, violent side… she'd never seen before.

He started toward her again, his blue eyes filled with anguish, but someone grabbed his arm.

Her hearing… her vision… all of her senses were bleary… and she felt faint. But she realized the man wore a police uniform and was talking sternly to Tal. Then handcuffs flashed.

Someone rested a hand on her and she jumped. But a calm, soothing female voice washed through her and the female officer guided Sonny with her to the car, saying something about getting her statement.

"Are you all right?" the woman asked. "Were you hurt?"

Tears flooded from her eyes as old pain, devastating and deep, surged to the surface.

"He raped me," she sobbed, covering her face with her hands.

Sonny sat in the chair beside the detective's desk. Someone had given her a blanket, which she clung to, holding it tightly around herself. Despite the fact it was a warm evening, she couldn't stop shivering.

"Sonny, are you okay?"

She glanced up at Steve's voice.

Steve hurried toward her, guided by the female officer. Sonny couldn't remember her name even though she'd introduced herself. Sonny had been having trouble focusing on anything they'd told her since they'd brought her here.

Detective Jenson, who'd been typing up a report on her computer, grabbed a chair for Steve.

"I'll get you both a coffee," she said and strode away.

"What are you doing here?" Sonny asked.

Steve sat down beside her, concern etched on his face.

"Tal called me. His lawyer's in talking to him now. He wanted me to check on you and make sure you get home okay."

"What about Tal?" she asked.

"Sonny, he's in some pretty deep trouble. The

police told me they arrested him for an unprovoked assault. Messed the guy up pretty badly."

She bit het lip, nodding.

"Sonny, is there anything you want to tell me?"

Her gaze turned to his and she trembled. She didn't want to talk about V, or explain why she knew him, or the reason Tal had attacked him.

"Sonny, the police told me you said he raped you."

She bit her lip and her gaze dropped to her hands.

"Sonny, look at me. Please."

She raised her gaze to his, his face a little fuzzy.

"I don't want to diminish what happened to you, or make you think I don't believe you, but I've known Tal a long time and I just don't understand—"

"Tal?" She stared at him, confused. Her head was spinning and she sucked in air.

"You said Tal raped you."

Her eyes widened and she felt faint. She grasped his arm, needing something to hold onto. Someone to hold onto.

"Not Tal. The other man."

All the swirling emotions… the violent memories… the fear… welled up inside her in an overwhelming maelstrom of fatigue, draining her of her last vestiges of strength. Everything around her faded to black.

Tal paced as he waited for Steve to return to the police station. All he could think about was the absolute terror in Sonny's eyes as she'd jerked away from him.

When he'd discovered the guy was one of the animals who had raped and beaten Sonny, he'd wanted to kill the guy. Probably would have if Sonny hadn't pulled him from his blind rage.

It had been his natural instinct to protect his woman. But what he had done was wrong. And the fact he'd frightened Sonny like that was indefensible.

He raked his hand over his close-cropped hair. What the hell had he been thinking? Not just when he went at the guy, but being involved with Sonny at all? She needed someone understanding and gentle. Someone she could feel safe with. How the hell could she feel safe with him when she knew he could fly into a rage and beat a guy to a pulp?

That violent nature that he'd thought he'd put behind him was obviously still very much a part of him.

He continued pacing. The detectives had been set to keep him in jail, but then he was told they were dropping the rape charge. He'd been shocked when his lawyer had told him that was one of the charges in the first place, but Sonny had been pretty disoriented—he could hardly blame her, coming face to face with one of the brutal men who had hurt her—so something she'd said must have been taken out of context.

His lawyer had arranged bail, but he had to wait for Steve. Finally, a policeman opened his cell and led him back to the front desk where Steve was waiting for him.

"Hey, sorry for taking so long."

"It's okay," Tal said. "Did Sonny get home okay?"

"Well, not exactly."

Tal's gaze shot to Steve.

"What do you mean *not exactly*?"

Steve's lips formed a tight line. "She's in the hospital."

"What the fuck? What happened?" His chest tightened.

"She was in pretty bad shape. When I got here and started talking to her, she seemed confused and disoriented. The police told me she said you raped her and that totally threw me. But when I asked her about it, she explained that she'd meant the guy you hit. I take it that's why you went at him."

Tal's gut clenched. "Yeah," he admitted. "But why's she in the hospital?"

"She was pretty traumatized. As we were talking, she fainted. I didn't realize what was happening until too late and she hit her head on the desk. Apparently, it happened because she went into shock, but now they think she might have a concussion, so they're keeping her in the hospital, at least overnight."

"Dammit. I want to go over there. Make sure she's okay."

"Of course. Let's go."

Sonny's head hurt. She'd just finished telling Leandra about seeing V and how that had caused the incident, then she'd found herself opening up to Leandra about the whole story of her past trauma. How she'd been kidnapped by the man who only went by D around her, and how she'd been used and abused by him and his friends. And that V had been one of them.

"Oh, my God, Sonny. I had no idea. No wonder you've always been so resistant when I try to set you up with a guy. I wish you'd told me."

"It's not something I like to talk about."

"No, of course." Leandra squeezed her hand. "Don't you know any of their names?"

"I didn't. I never knew where the house was. It could have been anywhere, since they drugged me when they took me there and when they got rid of me. The men were rich and they aren't in the public eye. I did searches on-line to try and find him, but I really didn't have enough to go on."

"You said you *didn't* know their names. You do now?"

"Just the guy called V. His name is Victor Langlon."

"Is he going to press charges against Tal?"

"They don't know yet. He's pretty banged up. He probably will."

Sonny's stomach clenched at the thought. Tal had reacted to the man's presence in a violent rage, but she knew it was because of his fury at the man hurting her. Tal wanted to protect and defend her. And now he would be punished.

"I talked to Detective Jenson about it and she said that they might have some leverage over V. They checked his background and found that another woman claimed he'd hurt her, too. Since it was going to be her word against his, with his resources and standing, she decided not to charge him, since there wasn't a hope she'd win. Detective Jenson thinks that with two of us now, though, they might be able to make a case. Even pressure him into giving up the identity of D so they can bring him in."

"That would be great. How do you feel about that?"

"Of course, I want to see D caught and punished, I'm just not up to thinking about what'll be involved in getting there right now."

The thought of having to relive the horror of the whole thing overwhelmed her.

"Yeah, of course." Leandra squeezed her hand again.

"Right now I'm worried about Tal. I don't want him go to prison for trying to protect me."

Tal walked into the hospital, Steve by his side, carrying the flowers he'd picked up on the way there. A mix of bright pinks and purples with sunny yellow accents. They stopped at the information desk to ask where to find her, then proceeded to her room.

He peered in the door and saw that Sonny already had a visitor. Her friend Leandra.

"Sonny, I know you're really taken by Tal," he overheard Leandra say, "which surprises me even more now that I know your story—"

"Tal isn't anything like those men."

"Maybe not, but he is violent. You saw the article. It's in his background and what happened tonight proves he's still like that."

"Leandra—"

"Honey, just let me finish. I'm just saying that

maybe you should move on. That man, Bryan, I set you up with really is perfect for you and I could tell there was some chemistry between you. If you tell him you have a trauma in your past and that you need to move really slowly, I know he'd be gentle and understanding. He'd be the perfect man to help you get over this."

Tal's chest constricted and he turned and walked away. Steve followed him.

"Tal," Steve said once they were out of earshot of the room, "I understand why you don't want to go in there right now, but we can wait until Leandra leaves, then you can go in and talk to Sonny."

Tal just shook his head as he stepped up to desk at the nurses' station and put down the flowers.

"Would you take these to room 404?" he asked the nurse there. "She has a visitor right now and I don't want to interrupt."

"Of course." The young green-eyed nurse smiled. "They're beautiful. I'm sure she'll love them."

Tal just nodded his thanks, then continued on his way, Steve following in his wake.

As soon as he opened the outside door and stepped into the fresh evening air, he breathed in deeply. He knew what he had to do. He wasn't the right man for Sonny. He knew it. Leandra knew it.

Now he had to make sure that Sonny understood it, too.

Sonny unlocked her apartment door and walked inside, Leandra on her heels. Mia sat on the carpet watching her come in, then stood up and walked away, stiff legged, making it clear she did not approve of Sonny's absence.

It had only been overnight, and Leandra had checked up on her, but Mia wasn't a cat to be reasoned with.

Sonny placed the two sets of flowers she'd received on the dining table. Some nice cut flowers from Leandra and the big, bright arrangement from Tal. She smiled as she rearranged some of the stems. A clear plastic holder displayed the simple get well card that Tal had simply signed, with no note. The nurse had said he'd been at the hospital to visit her but hadn't wanted to interrupt her visit with Leandra.

She wished he had come in. She really wanted to see him.

"Do you want me to stay and make lunch?" Leandra asked.

"No, I'm fine. They said I didn't have a concussion, remember?"

"I know, but you've been through a lot."

"I'm fine and I know you have to get back to work. I really appreciate you taking your lunch hour to drive me home."

Leandra hugged her. "Of course. That's what friends do." She glanced at her watch. "Okay, if you really don't need me for anything, I'll head back to the office. I'll call you tonight."

As soon as Leandra left, Sonny walked into the bedroom to find Mia. She was curled up on the bed and Sonny picked her up.

"Hey, there. Sorry I was gone last night."

She gave Mia a snuggle, but Mia wiggled until she worked her way free and bounded from her arms, then trotted off to the living room. Sonny walked to the kitchen, noticing that Mia was now perched on the top of her cat tree looking out the window.

She sighed. As she opened the fridge to see what she could pull together for lunch, someone knocked on the door. Had Leandra forgotten something?

She walked to the door and opened it.

Tal stood facing her.

Her whole mood brightened—it had taken a hit with Mia's rejection—and her lips turned up in a wide smile.

"Tal, I'm so glad to see you." She wanted to

throw herself into his arms, but his expression was guarded. He was probably worried about her.

"Come in," she said.

She stepped back, rather proud of herself that she didn't even think twice at asking him into her apartment. She'd come such a long way in a short time.

"Would you like to join me for lunch?" she asked.

"No, thanks. I heard you arrive and wanted to come by and see if you're okay."

"Yes. They discharged me this morning. I don't have a concussion." Her fingers drifted to the bandage on her head. "Just a cut and a bit of bruising. I feel fine."

"Good. I'm glad."

He sat down in the big armchair and she sat on the couch facing him. Immediately, Mia leaped from her cat tree and bounded onto Tal's lap. She curled up on his thick, muscular thigh and he stroked her furry body.

Sonny was jealous. Not because Mia chose to cuddle with Tal instead of her—that was Mia's way of punishing Sonny for leaving her alone—but because *she* longed to be on Tal's lap. And to feel his gentle strokes.

He pet Mia a little longer, then picked her up and set her on the floor, where she sauntered to the middle of the room and sat down to start licking her paw.

Tal leaned forward, resting his arms on his thighs, his hands folded. His expression was so serious a chill ran through her.

"Sonny, we need to talk."

Oh, God.

"Are you going to be charged with assault?" she asked.

"I don't know yet. One of the detectives is a friend of Steve's and he understands the situation, so they're going to do everything they can to help me out." He shook his head. "But that's not what I wanted to talk about."

"Okay."

"First, I want to apologize for that whole thing. I know that what I did made you uncomfortable. And it was wrong of me to physically assault someone. The thought of what he'd done to you drove me crazy and I just struck out. But that's no excuse. You, and how you were feeling, should have been my first and only concern."

"Oh, Tal. I understand. And I just hope you don't get charged—"

He raised his hand, his palm toward her.

"No. Don't let me off the hook. I grew up with violence and it seems I'll always be a violent man."

His clouded eyes, filled with pain, made her heart ache.

"Tal—"

"Let me finish this. You need to be with a man who is gentle. Who you can trust."

"I trust you."

His deep blue eyes turned to her, a fire blazing within.

"Well, you shouldn't," he snapped. "I'm bad news for you. Whether you know it or not, *I* know it. You need to find someone else to take you the rest of the way on your journey."

Shock surged through her.

His hands had balled into fists and there was anguish in his eyes. This wasn't easy for him. She could see that.

"I wish I could be the one to help you the rest of the way," he said, his voice softer, "I really do." He shook his head. "But I have to do what I think is best for you."

"Shouldn't I be the judge of that?" she asked.

"Not in this. So I'm ending whatever this is between us."

Her world came crashing down around her as she watched him.

He stood up and strode out the door. A moment later, she heard his apartment door close.

Oh, God, she'd lost him. The pain in her heart was almost unbearable.

He'd helped her on a healing journey past the worst trauma of her life. She'd opened up to him.

Shared intimacies she had started to doubt she'd ever share with a man again.

He said she should find someone else to help her on her journey, but how could she do that?

Since deep in her heart she knew… she was in love with Tal.

∾

Oh, God, her car wouldn't start. Sonny turned the key again, and gave it some gas. It made encouraging engine sounds… then died. Again.

The tension that had wound through her gut coiled tighter… tighter…tighter… then snapped.

She rested her head on the steering wheel, sucking in air.

This had been a lousy week. She felt like everything was falling apart around her.

She hit the dashboard with her fist, then cringed at the pain in her hand.

Then the tears let loose, streaming down her face.

She knew she should call Detective Jenson to say she'd be late, but right now the thought of doing anything was totally overwhelming. So she just sat there, letting her tears fall. Sucking in air between her shallow sobs.

Someone tapped on the window beside her. She

drew in a deep breath and lifted her head, then turned toward the sound.

"Sonny? You okay?" Tal asked, peering in at her.

Why did it have to be Tal? The sight of him made her heart ache so badly she could barely breathe.

She bit her lip, then pressed the button to open the window. But it didn't move. She grabbed a pack of tissues from the compartment between the seats and wiped her eyes, then she opened the door.

"The car won't start," she said through the crack in the door.

"Sonny, I find it hard to believe that you're this upset about your car not starting."

Her lips pursed. "Well, it's been a pretty brutal week."

His blue gaze, filled with sympathy, fell squarely on her."

"I know it has. Do you want me to take a look under the hood?" he asked.

She shook her head. "No, thanks. I have to be somewhere. I'll just have to Uber."

"No way. I'll drive you."

"You don't even know where I'm going."

"Doesn't matter."

He offered his hand to help her from the car. She didn't have the energy to be stubborn, so she took it. The feel of his big, warm hand around hers triggered a wild eruption of tingles quivering through her body.

She stepped out of the car and he led her through the shadowy underground parking to his car a few lanes over. When he released her hand to open the passenger door, she realized he'd held her hand all the way there.

But when he released it, she felt such an overwhelming sense of loss, she almost stumbled.

She got into the car and as soon as he sat in the driver's seat, she turned to him.

"I don't understand why you're doing this. You broke up with me."

"Doesn't mean I can't still be a good neighbor. And friend." His devastating blue eyes locked on her. "Sonny, I still care about you. I just don't think we should be together."

He started the car. "Now where to?"

Tal insisted on waiting while Sonny met with Detective Jenson. After the meeting, Tal stood up as she walked toward him, then he led her back to the car in silence, sensing her somber mood.

As soon as they were in the car, he turned to her.

"Do you want to tell me about it?"

She sighed, then told him about the other woman who'd been hurt by V.

"She wasn't one of D's captives," Sonny explained. "He asked her on a date and as soon as he got her alone, bound and brutalized her. The police want to use the threat of prosecuting him with what he did to both of us to try and get him to give up the name of the man who held me prisoner and some of the other men involved."

"That's good. That means they can find him and punish him. So why do you look so upset?"

"A little I'm worried that V will negotiate to be let off if he gives up the information they want, which means she won't see justice done. I don't know if that's likely to happen, but that would be awful for her... to get her hopes up that he might finally be punished, then have it torn away again."

He nodded. "What else?"

She stared at her hands as she fiddled with her fingers.

"I had to give Detective Jenson the details of what happened to me. How D kidnapped me. What he did afterward. She asked about the other men. Had me describe them. Tell him what they'd done to me."

She realized tears were trickling down her cheek.

"That must have been really hard, reliving it all again."

She sucked in a shaky breath, then lifted her gaze to his.

"It was." Her voice broke.

"Aw, fuck, Sonny." He wrapped his arms around her and pulled her close.

She rested her cheek against his muscular chest and soaked in the comfort of his embrace. His heartbeat—regular and soothing—thumped against her ear. She slid her arms around his waist and hung on tight to him.

Being this close to him… feeling his masculine heat…pulled her mind from the memory of the horrific experiences she had endured…reminding her of what it was like when she was with Tal. How different it was. How much she trusted him.

After a few moments passed, he squeezed her.

"Let's get you home."

She nodded then sat up. He started the car and soon they were on the road.

When they reached the apartment building, he went up with her instead of continuing with whatever errands he'd been going on earlier when he'd found her in her uncooperative car.

He stopped at his apartment door.

"Sonny, if you want to talk some more, or if you just don't want to be alone right now, you're welcome to come in."

She sent him a half-smile.

"I'd like that. Thank you."

She followed him into his apartment.

≈

Tal opened the door and led Sonny inside. He gestured for her to sit on the couch.

"I'll go make some herbal tea," he said, then strode into the kitchen and put the kettle on.

Knowing Sonny was hurting… that she'd had to relive those awful memories… made him ache inside. He wanted to do what he could to be there for her. To be supportive.

He dropped the tea bag into the pot.

But he also wanted to pull her into his arms and keep her close to him. To cradle her in his embrace. To kiss her. His body ached at the thought. To do whatever he could to wash away the memories that haunted her.

But he couldn't go down that path. Couldn't let himself be drawn into the desire for her that still burned fiercely inside him.

Even just holding her in the car had almost been his undoing.

The kettle boiled and he prepared the tea, then carried the two steaming mugs, into the living room and sat down beside Sonny on the couch.

Sonny sipped the fragrant blend, then set the mug on the coffee table.

"Sonny, if there's anything I can do… tonight or through the process… I'm here for you."

"Thank you." She rested her hand on his and he found himself taking it and squeezing it in his own.

They sat in silence for a few moments. He knew she probably didn't want to go back to her apartment and be alone with her thoughts, but he had no idea what to say to her. They were neighbors… and he hoped she considered him a friend… but the fact that they'd shared intimate encounters made it awkward. Especially since he'd ended that part of their relationship.

"Would you like me to put on a movie or something? Maybe order in a pizza?"

"No, thanks. I'm not really hungry and…" She lifted her gaze to his. "I'd really rather talk."

"Of course. What about?"

He doubted she wanted to talk about her past right now. Not after that session with the detective. But if she did, he'd listen.

"I guess it's not so much that I want to talk as… I'd like to ask a favor. You've helped me so much and I have no right to ask for any more, but…"

"What is it, Sonny?"

She bit her lip. "You said you don't think you're the one to help me with my intimacy problems."

"Sonny, please don't ask me to change my mind." It had been hard enough to break it off with her. To have her ask him to change his mind while she was so vulnerable would be devastatingly difficult.

She squeezed his hand. "I'm not asking you to get back together. It's just…"

As she gazed up at him, his heart ached.

"I feel comfortable with you. Last time, you let me see you… having pleasure."

Her wide eyes, so sweet and open, exposed her vulnerability.

"But I never got a chance to touch you. To know what it's like to feel you in my hands. To feel the pulsing need." She glanced downward. "I've been afraid to be with a man… to touch a man…I believe if I could take that step with you, I might not be so afraid. Then it would be easier to do it again. With someone else."

His stomach clenched at the thought of her doing it with anyone else.

Fuck, he didn't want her touching anyone but him. And he sure as hell didn't want another man touching her. Even thinking about it made him want to break the unknown guy's head open.

As the fierce thoughts surged through him, he fought to keep the darkness from his face. This was exactly why he couldn't continue with Sonny. He couldn't expose her to his violent disposition.

She gazed up at him again, her eyes filled with pleading.

"Please help me with this step."

His heart ached. He didn't want to walk away from her. He wanted to do everything he could to help her past her trauma. And, goddammit, he wanted to touch her. To know what it felt like to stroke her soft breasts. To feel her quivering in his arms.

But he had to put those urges aside. For her own good.

But now she was asking a favor. To let *her* touch him.

How could he do that without wanting… *needing*… more?

"You're asking to touch my cock?"

She drew in a breath and nodded.

Fuck, the thought of her touching him with her soft hands… stroking his hard flesh… had his cock pulsing with need.

"Sonny, I don't intend to have sex with you, so if you're just trying—"

"No, I'm not. I'm asking for your help." Her lips turned up in a small, uncertain smile. "I promise, I won't take advantage of you."

His somberness melted away and he chuckled.

"Shouldn't that be my line?" he asked.

Fuck, he wanted this as much as she did. He'd just have to rein in his need. He would *not* allow this to go too far.

"All right."

Sonny's stomach fluttered as she took his hand and stood up. This was a little scary, but it also excited her tremendously.

"Where's the bedroom?" she asked as she glanced around the apartment.

He squeezed her hand. "Whoa. I don't think the bedroom is a good idea. The couch will be fine."

She turned to him. "I promised you I wouldn't take advantage of the situation. You trust me, don't you?"

"Yes, of course, but… why the bedroom?"

"I want to be where you would usually be when you… pleasure yourself. I want to imagine what it would be like if you took me in there and…"

Her words trailed off. He watched her face, considering, then finally drew in a deep breath.

"Yeah, okay. I get it."

He stood up and led her down a short hallway to his bedroom.

It was tidy and masculine. He'd painted two of the walls a rich russet red, and the bed-covering was a navy print with the same russet color running through the pattern. He walked to the bed and sat on the side.

"You want me to lie down, right?" he said.

She walked to the bed and propped up his

pillow, then grabbed the second one. She plumped it up and set it on top.

"You can sit up," she said.

He shifted onto the bed and stretched out, leaning back against the pillows.

"Okay, here I am."

She bit her lip. "Would you mind taking off your T-shirt?"

He gazed at her, his eyes assessing. Then he reached for the hem of his shirt, tugged it over his head and tossed it aside.

The sight of his broad, sculpted chest and his bulging muscular arms was breathtaking, especially covered with the detailed tattoos. Her gaze glided down his stomach to the tight ridges of his abs. Then to his jeans. There was already a bulge forming there.

"Do you want me to unzip and pull it out?" he asked.

Her gaze jumped back to his face.

"No, I'd like to do it in my own time." She needed to ease into this.

As she took in the sight of his magnificent shoulders, she noticed a line on his upper right arm that seemed to slice through the tattoos. She sat down on the bed and looked closer. It was a scar.

She rested her finger on it tentatively, then traced the line.

"Did your stepfather do this?"

"Yeah. I told you he got a few slashes in before I could stop him."

She traced her finger lightly, back and forth, imagining the pain he must have felt.

Knowing that the most painful scars he carried were much deeper than this.

She slid her hand from his shoulder to his chest, flattening her palm over his heart. She could feel it beating.

Then she slid downward, over the hard muscles of his abs. Stopping at the top of his jeans.

She gazed at his face, his deep blue eyes fixed on her intently.

She unfastened the button, drawing in slow, deep breaths to keep herself calm.

This was so strange. Being in a man's bedroom. Touching his body.

Undoing his pants.

Even a week ago, she would never have imagined herself in this position.

But meeting Tal had changed everything.

She pulled down the zipper of his jeans, watching the fabric part. Sucking in a breath at the size of the ridge inside.

She hooked her finger under the elastic of his underwear and slowly drew it down.

Her breathing stopped as she revealed the huge, mushroom-shaped tip. As she continued to pull down the fabric, she marveled at the breadth of his big shaft.

His cock was proportionate to the size of his body… which meant it was massive.

Mesmerized, she ran the tip of her finger along the hot, hard flesh. It swelled bigger and rose upward.

He shifted, pushing down his jeans and underwear, then kicking them away. He sat more upright against the pillows, his cock angled away from his body now rather than standing straight up.

"There you go, sweetheart. You have full access."

Oh, God, it looked even bigger now. He had his legs parted, so she could see his big testicles hanging between his legs.

She slid onto the bed beside him, looking at it from the same angle as him. Then she pushed herself onto her knees and curled her fingers under it, cradling the long thick shaft in her hands.

It was heavy and hot. She could feel it pulsing in her hands.

She wanted to wrap her fingers around it and stroke, like he had done when he'd shown her how he gave himself pleasure.

But right now she just wanted to look at it, and enjoy the feel of it against her palms.

She licked her lips, realizing that even more, she wanted to taste it.

She leaned forward and ran her tongue over the tip.

~

At the first touch of her damp, warm tongue, a burning need careened through Tal from every extremity right to his core. As she lapped delicately on the tip of him in growing circles, the need inside him burned with the heat of a thousand suns.

She moved her head and he felt her tongue at his root, gliding upward, like he was a lollipop.

She licked his length several times, then turned and stared at him. Her eyes were so full of need he thought he'd explode.

She shifted her body, moving between his knees and facing him. Her gaze turned back to his aching cock. His pulse raced as she wrapped her small hands around his shaft. She leaned forward and her tongue curled under the swell of his corona and glided around it, circling his cockhead with delicate strokes.

"Ah, fuck, baby. That feels so good."

Her gaze shifted to his and the heat crackling between them took his breath away.

She suckled the side of his cockhead, making him long to be fully in her mouth. He rested his hand on her head, stroking her hair back, the long blonde strands coiling around his fingers.

Her tongue laved over him, swirling around the tip first, then the circles growing bigger.

When she opened her lips around him, he didn't think she'd be able to get his cock into her mouth. Many women had trouble with that and Sonny was petite. But she glided her lips downward, opening wider and wider.

He watched her, amazed and wildly turned on, as she continued downward until she took the whole cockhead in her mouth.

Oh, fuck, the feel of her around him was heaven.

When she glided even further, he groaned.

Her hands started to move up and down. She moved deeper on him, taking in almost half his shaft. Her hands clung tight to the rest of it.

When she started to move her hands and mouth in unison, up and down his aching cock, he nearly choked with need.

Oh, God, the feel of his massive cock pulsing in her hands… filling her mouth… had her body quivering with need. What would it feel like to have him inside her body? The big shaft gliding deep into her. Stretching her with his hefty girth.

She could feel the melting flesh between her legs. She knew she was so wet she could climb on top of him right now and take him inside with no problem.

And, oh, God, she wanted to so badly.

If she stripped off her clothes right now, she was sure he wouldn't stop her if she slid onto his lap and pressed his big cockhead to her slickness, then lowered herself onto him.

But trust went both ways and she'd promised him she wouldn't take advantage.

Even begging him to make love to her now wouldn't be fair. Convincing herself it would then be his decision was just a lie. He'd said at the outset that he didn't want to go any further than this and she had to honor that.

So she sucked him deeply then surged downward, taking him as far as she could.

Dark thoughts on the edge of her consciousness… about how she'd become so good at this… tried to push forward, but she stifled them.

This was Tal, and she *wanted* to be with him. *Wanted* to give him pleasure.

"Sonny, are you okay?"

She gazed up at his deep blue eyes, filled with concern.

She loved touching his naked body. Loved his thick cock filling her like this.

She drew back. "I'm fine. I'm just so happy you're letting me do this."

He looked doubtful and she was sure he'd seen the dark cloud of the past in her eyes.

She filled her mouth with his big member again, and then slid her fingers under one of his big balls and caressed it, to his groan.

She suckled and squeezed his cockhead, then glided her tongue down his length and lapped at his balls. Then she drew one into her mouth, cradling it gently.

"Ohhhh, baby." His hand cupped her head and he stroked her hair gently.

She massaged his soft flesh with her tongue, then lightly suckled, her hand gliding up and down his erection.

"Fuck, baby, you've got me so hot."

She stroked faster, pumping him in deep strokes. Imagining that big cock inside her body. Filling her with pleasure.

"I'm so fucking close."

She licked up his cock again and gazed into his eyes, her hand snug around his shaft, her lips poised on his tip.

"Come for me," she said.

Then she dove down deep. She pumped him with her mouth, moving up and down, taking him deep.

She felt his body tense. Then he groaned and hot liquid squirted deep into her throat.

She kept sucking and pumping, milking every

last drop from him.

When he was done, she kept him in her mouth a moment longer, not wanting this intimacy to end. She caressed his hot flesh with her tongue, stroking it lovingly.

Finally, she eased back, slipping his giant cock from her lips.

She slid up beside him on the bed and snuggled in close, her legs curled beside her as she wrapped one arm around his waist and the other around his bulging, muscular arm and rested her head on his shoulder.

He was still sucking in air, his head resting against the pillows, his eyes closed.

She ran her hand down his naked chest, the solid muscle rock hard under her fingertips. His skin was glazed with a thin layer of sweat.

A deep longing throbbed inside her and she yearned for him to roll over and take her. To plunge deep inside her and sate this heart-rending ache.

She sighed, allowing her hand to stray to his cheek, then gently stroke his face.

"Thank you, Tal."

He chuckled, a rumble from deep inside his massive chest.

"You just gave me the best orgasm of my life and you're thanking *me*?"

She nuzzled his jawline, loving the raspy feel of his coarse whiskers against her lips. She dragged her teeth over his chin. The feel of the thick stubble against her teeth was intensely masculine.

Tal curled his hand over her shoulder and eased her back.

"Sonny, it's not going any further than this."

She drew in a deep breath and sighed. "I know."

She ran her fingertips along his temple and around his ear, wanting so badly to pull him in for a kiss. But instead she slumped against his side, tightening her arm around his waist again, unwilling to let him go just yet.

Fuck, he realized that she was aroused and needy right now, but there wasn't anything he could do to help her with that. Because he knew if he opened that door, he wouldn't be able to stop himself.

He'd take her.

All the way.

Once he started down that path, the only thing that would stop him would be her. If she said 'no' at any step along the way, he'd back right off. No matter how difficult it might be.

But he knew she wouldn't.

"I'm sorry, Sonny. I shouldn't have said yes to this. Now you want more and—"

"No, it's okay. I'm glad you said yes. I wanted

this. And I meant it when I said I wouldn't take advantage."

She eased away and he immediately wished he could pull her back against him.

"I do have another favor to ask of you, though," she said.

His mouth turned up in a half grin. "I thought you said you weren't going to take advantage."

She bit her lip and her big, brown eyes filled with anxiety.

Shit, now he felt like a jerk. "Sonny, it's okay. I was just joking."

He sat up more and took her hand. "Please tell me what it is."

She frowned, but nodded.

"Since you've decided that…" She sucked in a breath. "Since you and I will never make love… I was hoping you would make another audio for me. Where we… actually do it together. Where you describe how you'd make love to me. How it would feel. What you'd do. What you'd like me to do."

Fuck. Just the thought sent his head spinning. If he sat in his apartment, thinking about how he'd touch her… recording his voice as he imagined stripping her down… touching her soft, beautiful body… then sliding his cock into her velvety opening…

His cock was swelling at the images fluttering

through his brain, and since it was exposed, it was excruciatingly obvious.

Her gaze shifted to his solid shaft rising upward.

"You clearly want to." Her gaze returned to his face. "Please, Tal. If I can never experience it in real life, at least give me that."

"Fuck, baby, I…"

But she wrapped her hand around him and stroked. He groaned.

"You're not playing fair, baby," he murmured.

She nodded, then leaned down and licked him, her soft tongue sending heat crackling through him.

"I know. Because I really want this."

He drew her toward him and, unable to resist, pulled her into a kiss. Her tongue greeted his as he pushed inside her sweet mouth. As he deepened the kiss, pulling her tight to his chest, he drew her hand from his cock.

He released her lips. "Okay, I'll do it. But you're leaving now."

Tal sat and stared out the window over his desk at the great view of the river and park. He was too distracted to get much work done this after-noon. Maybe going for a walk in the bright summer sunshine would help him regain his focus.

But what was really preoccupying him was the promise he'd made to Sonny a few days ago to make the audio. Fuck, anytime he started to think about doing it, he got so turned on he could barely think straight, let alone figure out a coherent set of things to say.

She wanted to have sex with him, which was amazing. It was a huge step forward for her. And he sure as hell wanted to have sex with her. Why the hell was he holding back? Had he been a fucking idiot to break it off with her?

But the image of her frightened face when he'd attacked the guy who'd hurt her still haunted him. He never wanted to see that look on her face again. The fact that he had triggered it tore him in two.

His hands clenched into fists. He wanted so badly to be the first man she made love with since her ordeal. He wanted to show her such sweet tenderness and caring that she'd never fear being with a man again.

Fuck, who was he kidding? He wanted her to want to be with him. And him alone.

Because he had fucking fallen in love with her.

A rapping at the apartment door broke Tal's

reverie. He pushed his chair back from the desk and strode to the entrance. Sonny's beautiful face greeted him as he opened the door.

"Hi," he said.

"Hi." Her face glowed as her lips turned up in a smile. "May I come in?"

"Uh… yeah, sure."

"I wanted to update you on what's happening," she said, as she followed him into the living room.

She sat down on the couch and he sat across from her, not wanting to be too close.

"Good news?" he asked.

"They found another woman who wants to press charges against V. They've arrested him. But they also found he's had some shady financial dealings. They're offering him a deal to reduce the charges on that if he confesses to the sexual assault charges and gives them enough information to make a case against D."

"That is good news."

She nodded. "Not only that, he told them D's identity and the location of the house where he'd kept me. When the police showed up there, they found he had another woman held captive."

"Fuck." Anger flared through Tal.

She nodded. "She'd been there a week, but they were able to get her out before she suffered months of brutality."

She stood up and walked toward him and sat

down on the arm of his chair, then took his hand. The gentle touch of her fingers made his heart thump faster.

"And it's all because of you. You're a hero."

"No. Assaulting someone… terrifying you… those are not heroic acts."

"Tal, you're beating yourself up more about this than you beat him. He did far worse to me, and who knows how many other women."

Tal's heart clenched at her words, terrible images of Sonny beaten and in pain surging through him.

"I was terrified when I saw him… frozen to the spot," she continued. "If you hadn't shown up when you did, he would have continued on his way and we never would have found out his identity. The police would never have arrested him, and they wouldn't have found D and saved the new woman he kidnapped."

She squeezed his hand.

"Don't you see, Tal? You saved me from the endless fear of knowing he's still out there free. Maybe coming back for me. You've saved V's victims from the same fear. And you've saved countless women who might have become future victims if these men weren't found and, hopefully, locked up for a long time."

She rested her soft hand on his cheek.

"You're so hard on yourself, but you are a

sweet, caring man. The fact that you struck out at him was a reaction to the horrible things he'd done, and your deep need to protect me, which is a wonderful thing. Please don't judge yourself badly for one extreme, emotional act."

Her fingers glided over his jaw. Her tender touch, and the sight of her large, luminous brown eyes gazing at him with gratitude and… something deeper… made his heart swell.

If this woman could accept him exactly as he was, then… maybe he wasn't the violent animal he'd always feared he was.

He pulled her onto his lap and kissed her. The feel of her lips, so soft and pliant under his, filled him with a growing desire.

When he eased back, she gazed up at him with a smile.

"Tal, have you made that audio for me yet?"

Sonny watched Tal blink in confusion and she laughed.

"The audio?" he asked.

"That's right." She rested her hand on his chest and stroked gently. "Because if you haven't… maybe you could do it now."

"Now? With you here, you mean?"

Heat shimmered through her body.

"Yes. With me right here."

He slid her off his lap and stood up, then he strode down the hall and disappeared.

She stared after him, confused. Was that a no? Did he expect her to leave now?

But he returned a moment later with a laptop and microphone in his hand. He set it down on the table beside the couch and opened the computer, then connected the microphone and set it on a stand beside it.

"Sit in the chair," he instructed.

She sat down in the armchair across from the couch, watching him open an app on the computer and then he sat down on the couch.

He grabbed the hem of his white t-shirt and pulled it over his head, then tossed it to the floor. She almost gasped at the sensational sight of his glorious muscles and dense tattoos.

He closed his eyes, and drew in a few deep breaths. She licked her lips, longing to cross the distance between them and sit down beside him, then stroke that incredible chest.

After a few moments, he opened his eyes.

His gaze locked on her and glided down her body. She felt heat swelling inside her at his potent male attention. His focus shifted to her breasts and she found herself intensely conscious of her breathing, Of the rise and fall of her chest.

His blue eyes darkened to the color of the

midnight sky and she noticed the bulge forming in his jeans. His hand rested on it and he began to stroke.

"You're sure you're ready for this?" he asked.

The sight of his hand gliding over the denim… stroking his cock… made her stomach flutter. Desire washed through her.

She stared at him, mesmerized.

"Uh huh," she said weakly.

His lips curled up in a broad smile. "Okay."

He clicked a button on the laptop, then leaned back on the couch. His gaze settled on her face.

Hello, baby. I've been sitting here thinking about you. About what it would be like to make love to you.

I want to know what it would feel like to touch you. To cup your soft, naked breasts in my hands. Feel your nipples pucker and harden against my palms.

His gaze dropped to her breasts, sending need surging through her. She wanted his hands on her so badly.

Mmm. I'm getting hard just thinking about it. My cock is swelling inside my jeans.

In my fantasy, you lean forward in the big armchair and smile as you run your hands down your body…

*then grasp the hem of your shirt and draw it up...
Slowly… Seductively…*

She ran her fingers down the side of her shirt, then slowly started pulling it up, her deep need to be with him compelling her to bring this fantasy to life. His deep blue eyes flared with heat.

Fuck, seeing more and more of your naked skin being exposed is making me rock hard. I'm stroking my cock as you pull your top all the way off.

She drew in a breath and tugged it off, tingles dancing across her skin as his gaze lingered on her breasts.

Oh, yeah. I love your sheer, black lace bra that barely covers your nipples.

She watched his hand stroke over the front of his jeans. She sucked in a breath, wishing she was feeling what his fingers felt right now.

Ah, fuck, baby, you are so sexy.

I imagine you standing up and unzipping your jeans then dropping them to the floor.

Mesmerized by the longing in his eyes, she

stood up and unzipped her pants, then sucked in a breath and dropped them to the floor.

He smiled.

Mmm, now you're standing in front of me in just your sexy bra and those tiny matching panties.

You slowly walk toward me, then kneel in front of me and watch my hand gliding over my growing bulge.

She stepped out of her jeans, then knelt in front of him, her gaze locked on his moving hand.

Ah, baby. The thought of you close to me… watching me… is driving me wild. I ache to feel your hands on me. Your lips.

I know you want to touch me. To taste me.

Your hand glides up my thigh over the denim. Slowly. Building up my need until it's a desperate ache inside me.

She rested her hand on his warm thigh, then moved along it, watching his hand moving, along his shaft, wishing it was her hand around it.

When you finally reach my cock, you stroke along the swollen shaft, squeezing it through the denim.

She gazed into his eyes, her heart pounding as he slid his hand away. She drew in a deep breath and glided over his thick bulge. Oh, God it was so hard.

Unzip my jeans, baby, and pull it out.

She drew in a breath and unzipped him, then reached inside. As her fingers wrapped around his rigid cock, the heat of it made her melt. She drew it out and stared at it. It was gigantic. Swollen and red, with veins throbbing along the sides. The head was as large as a plum. She wanted to lick it.

Ohhh, yeah, the feel of your fingers around me is making me harder. And the way you're looking at my cock… as if you want to devour me… You're making me so fucking hot.

Can you feel me pulsing in your hand?

God, yes, she could. It sent quivers through her.

Now you're stroking me. Your hand gliding my length.

She stroked his shaft, loving the feel of him in her grip. Heat pulsed through her as she longed to feel him inside her.

Mmm, baby. I love that.

You lean forward and press your lips to my cock. Your tongue laps over the tip. Can you taste the salty precum?

Her gaze locked on the shiny droplet and she licked her lips. Then she leaned forward and pressed her mouth to him, his rigid flesh hot against her. When she licked, she did taste his salty essence.

Your mouth opens around me… gliding down… taking my whole cockhead inside.

She slid down on him. He was so thick and hard. She squeezed him between her lips as she started to move up and down.

Mmm, I love feeling your warm lips moving up and down on me.

Ah, baby, it feels so good when you squeeze me like that.

Oh, yeah. As you take me deeper, I feel my groin tighten.

She glided all the way down, taking his entire length down her throat. He groaned.

Fuck, I can't believe how deep you can take me.

I coil my hand in your hair and draw your head back until only my cockhead is in your tight, warm grip.

She felt his hand grasp her hair, then the gentle tug as he wrapped it around his hand and drew her back.

Suck me, baby.

Her gaze locked on his deep blue eyes, she suckled lovingly on his cockhead, to his soft moan.

Ah, yeah, that feels so good. I'm getting so fucking close.

He throbbed within her grip. She tucked her hand inside his jeans and cupped his balls.

Mmm. With you stroking me like that… your hot mouth gripping me so tightly… You're taking me too close to the edge.

I want to be inside you when I come. Sheathed in your sweet pussy.

You want that, too. I can see it in your eyes. So hot and hungry.

She nodded, her body aching for the feel of his thick cock deep inside her.

Stand up, baby. Take off your bra and let me see your beautiful breasts.

She released his massive erection and stood up, then reached behind her.

That's right. I can hardly wait to see them.

As her bra slid from her body, his eyes darkened to the color of the midnight sky.

Oh, yeah. You are so fucking sexy. I want to touch you so badly.

She bit her lip. She'd touched *him*, but she'd never felt his hands on her body. Touching her intimately.

But, oh, God, she wanted to.

And I can see the need in your eyes. You want my hands on you, don't you?

She nodded. A smile spread across his face and his big hand covered her breast.

She sucked in a breath at the intensity of the emotions surging through her. A touch of fear quickly crushed by a need so intense, she felt she'd die if she denied herself.

I cup your breast and... Ah, fuck, baby. You're so incredibly soft.

The warmth of his strong hand around her, combined with the awe and tenderness in his voice, mirrored in his dark blue eyes, made her eyes well with tears.

He cupped her other breast, too, then gently stroked them.

I'm touching both your breasts now. Do you like the feel of me caressing you like this?

Pleasure rippled through her in waves.
"Yes. Oh, God, I love you touching me."
His soft laugh curled through her.

That's good. Because I love touching you.

His thumbs found her nipples and glided over them, to her soft moans.

Mmm, your nipples are so hard. Do you like me stroking them like this? Squeezing them?

She whimpered as she nodded.

Fuck, it's making me hard as a rock.

I'm pulling you closer and swirling my tongue over your swollen nub. Suckling it until you arch against me, moaning for more. Then I suck it deep into my mouth.

He leaned forward and lapped his tongue over her nipple, but then drew back. She moaned at the loss. Oh, God, she needed so much more from him.

Are you wet for me, baby?

I'm sliding my hand inside your panties. I want to feel your slick flesh.

His gaze locked on hers, questioning as his hand slid down her stomach then stopped at the top of her panties. She bit her lip, hunger burning through her, and nodded.

His fingers slid beneath the fabric.

At the feel of his fingers gliding over her slick folds, her insides melted and pleasure spiked through her.

Ohhh, baby. You are wet.

Her heart ached at how gentle his touch was. How tender the look in his eyes.

Mmm. Knowing you want me so badly has me aching inside. I desperately want to fill you with my throbbing cock. To be surrounded by your warm, velvety pussy.

His fingers kept moving on her. Then they slipped inside her opening.

"Oh, God, Tal."

A moan vibrated from her lips.

Do you want me inside you? Do you want to feel my thick, hard cock glide into you?

"Oh, yes! Please," she whimpered.

He chuckled softly.

Take off your panties. Show me that sweet pussy of yours.

She stood up, then pushed them down. His appreciative gaze lit a fire inside her.

Ohhh, so beautiful. Come here, baby. On my lap.

She knelt on the couch facing him, her legs straddling his thighs.

I'm brushing my cockhead over your slick opening. Ohhh, that feels so fucking good.

The feel of his hot, rigid flesh touching her there made her feel weak.

Fear reared up. She hadn't had a man touch her like this since…

But she gazed into his deep blue eyes and saw the sweet tenderness there.

It's okay, baby. You're safe with me.

She knew she was. This was Tal. He wouldn't hurt her. She nodded.

You take the lead. We'll go as fast or as slow as you want.

She drew in a breath, then slowly lowered her body. The feel of his cockhead stretching her made her tense, but he stroked her back tenderly and his eyes were filled with encouragement.

That's right, baby. Slide your pussy down on me.

She took him deeper. Oh, God, she couldn't

believe he was inside her. Her heart pounded as heat surged through her.

His face filled with awe and wonder as she took him all the way inside. His groans of pleasure sent tremors through her.

Ohhh, the feel of you around me… so warm and welcoming… Ohhh, fuuuuck.

Goddamn. I can't believe I'm all the way inside you.

His hands gripped her hips, holding her tight to his groin, as he stared into her eyes.

Do you like the feel of my cock inside you? Pulsing with need?

"Oh, yes," she whimpered.

God, I need to fuck you now. Rock against me, baby. I want to feel my cock drive deep into you.

She rocked and he thrust forward, driving his cock deeper.

His hands grasped her hips and he guided her to keep rocking. She moaned at the joy surging through her.

Oh, you feel so good.

Your moans are driving me wild. I'm so fucking close.

But I'm not going to come until you do. I want to see your face as I make you come.

He ground forward, making her whimper at the intense pleasure. Then he started gliding into her in deep strokes.

That's right, baby. Feel my cock moving deep inside you. Squeeze it tight.

She squeezed and he groaned.

Oh, fuck yeah.

His sounds of pleasure vibrated through her

I'm thrusting into you now.

He thrust deep again and again. She felt like she was riding a wild stallion, as he pumped into her in a steady, pulsing rhythm. Driving her pleasure higher.

You like this, baby? My cock gliding in and out of your pussy?

"Ohhh, yes."

Ahhh, I'm so close. I can barely hold back. I'm going to stroke your clit now, baby.

His hand slid down her stomach and his finger found her clit. She sucked in a breath as his finger teased over it. Pleasure blossomed inside her.

Yeah, there it is. I'm stroking your hard clit. You like that, don't you?

Fuck, your whimpers are… ohh… so sweet.

Come for me.

He thrust deep again and joy burst through her, catapulting her over the edge. She began to trill, then moaned loudly as he continued to fill her with his hard cock. Pleasure rocked her world, filling her with ecstasy.

Oh, fuck, baby! Ohhh, fuuuuck!

His voice pulsed as he thrust into her.

That's… right… Fuck… you're… so… beautiful.

Ohhh, God… you feel… so good.

Ohhh, fuck… Ohhh, fuuuck, yeah… Ohhh, I'm…
ahhhh… fucking coming.

His intense groans of pleasure pushed her bliss
even higher. Then he drove deeper and shuddered
against her.

Ahhhh, baby. Oh, goddamn.

He drew in thick, heavy breaths as she rested
against him. Slowly his breathing calmed.

Oh, fuck. That was incredible. You were incredible.

His muscular arms tightened around her and he
hugged her snug to his body. The feel of his tender
embrace, his cock still embedded inside her, made
her glow with happiness.

Thank you, baby.

Tal's heart pounded as he held Sonny close to him.
The experience had left him deeply moved. This
woman, who had been hurt so heinously, had
opened up to him. Had trusted him so completely.

He could feel Sonny trembling in his arms. He
brushed his lips against her temple.

"You okay, sweetheart?"

He felt dampness against his chest and his heart clenched. He tipped up her chin to see her eyes gleaming with moisture.

"Sonny?"

"I'm just so…" Her eyes filled with deep emotion. "It was just so…"

She shook her head and cupped his face with both hands, then surged forward, capturing his lips. Her sweet mouth moved on his, her tongue gliding inside, exploring.

When she released him and gazed into his eyes, he realized it was joy she was feeling.

"So it was good."

Her lips turned up in a smile, her face glowing, then she laughed. At the same time, tears streamed from her eyes.

"It was *very* good."

He laughed, then swept her into his arms and carried her to his bedroom. He pushed back the covers and laid her on the bed, then dropped his jeans to the floor and slid in beside her. The feel of her naked body against his, the two of them warm and snug together, sent his heart soaring. She wrapped her arms around his waist and cuddled closer, her soft cheek against his bare chest, her hair a silken caress against his skin.

She sighed contentedly and soon her slow, deep breaths told him she'd fallen asleep.

He tightened his arms around her, never wanting this moment to end.

Sonny awoke to the muted light of late afternoon, casting long shadows across the bed.

Tal's big muscular arms were around her, his heart beating against her ear. She stared at the dense tattoos on his chest, smiling at the memory of what they'd done. At the tender way Tal had guided her past her carefully erected barriers.

How he'd gently helped her shed her last fear of making love with a man.

She dragged a finger down the curved line of one of his tattoos.

At least, a man she trusted as much as Tal.

"You're awake." Tal's voice rumbled from deep in his chest.

She smiled, and gazed up into his dark blue eyes.

"Yes. And so are you."

"You do realize you're naked?"

"Really?" She lifted the covers and peered underneath, seeing her breasts pressed against his sexy, muscular-ridged chest. "You're right." She leaned back to gaze at his boxers. "But you're not. That seems wholly unfair."

He chuckled. "I can fix that."

As he tucked his thumbs under the waistband of his boxers and started to guide them down, she knew exactly where this was headed. Her heart pounded in anticipation. But she grasped his hands and stopped him, knowing she had to talk to him first.

"Wait," she said.

He stopped and glided a big hand down her back in a tender stroke.

"What is it, baby?"

"We need to talk."

The light in his eyes dimmed, but he nodded. "Of course. Whatever you want."

"First, I want to say I'm sorry."

He frowned, looking perplexed. "Sorry? For what?"

"You told me you didn't want to continue this relationship with me... that you didn't want to go further on this journey. Yet I went ahead and pushed you into doing this."

"I didn't say I didn't want to help you. I said I was the wrong man for the job."

She nodded. "Yes, but..."

She rested her hand on his cheek and stroked, loving the feel of his coarse stubble. God, he was so intensely masculine.

He took her hand and pressed the palm to his lips, making her quiver.

"But what, baby?"

127

"I'm hoping you'll reconsider. Continuing this relationship I mean."

"Why?"

Her heart stuttered. Oh, God. She'd begun to hope he wanted her. That him agreeing to do the audio with her then the two of them making love, meant that he had changed his mind. But maybe he'd just relented to help her past this one major hurdle and he intended to just walk away again.

She choked up, realizing he probably felt there were no more steps for him to help her through. Going forward, she needed to find a way to build trust with a man and if Tal didn't plan to be in a long-term relationship with her, then it was time for her to move on and learn how to do that with someone else.

The problem was, she didn't want anyone else.

She wanted Tal.

He watched the emotions washing across her face and… Oh, God… she realized he was going to be *kind*.

She drew back, her head shaking, knowing she had to flee. But he tightened his arms around her, pulling her close again.

"Where are you going?"

"If you don't want to be with me then…" her throat choked and she sucked in a breath. "I should go."

He rolled her onto her back, pinning her hands

beside her head, his solemn blue eyes searching hers.

"You think I don't want you? You *were* in the fucking room, weren't you?" His voice—low, sexy and with the hint of a growl—rippled through her.

His mouth swooped down and his lips coaxed hers with such poignant persuasion that she opened, melting into the kiss. His tongue explored her mouth, insistent and possessive.

"Baby, I've never wanted a woman more." His gruff, sexy voice rumbling against her ear melted her heart. "And I don't mean because of the sex." He nipped her earlobe. "Though there's no denying the chemistry between us. But I mean I want you as a part of my life. Today. Tomorrow. And as long as you'll have me."

Her eyes widened and her lips parted in awe. He captured her mouth for another passionate kiss, then gazed at her with a tenderness that filled her with awe.

"Fuck, baby, I'm so in love with you I never want to let you go."

Tal watched Sonny's face. Had he said too much too fast?

When he'd asked her why she wanted him to reconsider continuing the relationship, he'd been

OPAL CAREW

hoping she would say because she loved him. He'd been a fool to believe that might be possible. Not so quickly.

Grateful, yes. But she probably wasn't ready to love anyone yet.

"You're in love with me?" she whispered.

"Yes, baby." He watched a light flare in her eyes.

But then her lip trembled and he was afraid—

"Oh, Tal. I love you, too."

Joy surged through him. He couldn't believe his dream had come true. He meshed his lips with hers and she kissed him with sweet exuberance.

When their lips finally parted, she laughed.

"Tal, you need to let me go."

He realized he still had her wrists pinned.

"Why? Is there somewhere you want to go?"

She wriggled beneath him, the movement of her naked body sending all kinds of delightful signals through his body. He released her hands.

"No. Nowhere I want to go." She pressed a hand to his chest until he rolled away, and she rolled right on top of him. She rose onto her knees. "There's something I want to do."

She grasped his boxers and pulled them down, freeing his rising cock, then tugged them down his legs, stripping them away entirely. Then she prowled up his body, her eyes filled with hunger.

When her hand wrapped around his cock, he

groaned with need. But he caught her wrist and rolled her onto her back again.

"Oh no you don't. You've had your turn. Twice. Now it's mine."

"But—"

He consumed her mouth, silencing her, then kissed down her neck.

"Every time we've been together, you've ensured you kept me busy talking," he murmured against her skin as he nuzzled her neck, then continued downward. "So I was never able to taste you the way I wanted to."

He cupped her breast and stare at the peaked nipple, so long and hard. He smiled, then licked it.

"Now I'm going to feast on you to my heart's content."

He wrapped his lips around her rosy areola and suckled softly. Her sweet moans made his cock swell until it was rock hard. Her fingers stroked over his head, then wrapped around it as she pulled him tight to her, arching against his mouth.

He laughed, rumbling from his chest, then drew deep on the hard nub.

"Oh, Tal. Yes."

Her throaty voice, so filled with need, sent his cock twitching. Aching to be inside her.

He captured her other nipple and lapped at it with his tongue, then drew it into his mouth and sucked with a deep, pulsing rhythm. Her moans turned to high, trilling cries.

He flicked his tongue over her hard nub, then glided his lips down her ribs, directly to her navel, then he dabbed his tongue inside the small indent. His hand glided down her sides to her hips, her skin silky under his fingertips.

Then he drew back and took in the sight of her body in front of him. His gaze gliding down her stomach to the neatly trimmed, silky blonde curls of her pussy. He ran his fingertip along one side. Then the other. He smiled and used his thumbs to open the folds, ready to lick her delightful, sensitive flesh.

"Tal…"

He gazed up at her face. "What is it, sweetheart?"

"I've never had a man… do that."

"Really, baby?"

He pushed himself up on his elbows, their gazes locked.

"I'd… only been with one guy before I was… abducted. And he didn't do that with me. And D and the others…"

Tal surged upward and captured her lips. "It's okay, baby. You're here now. You're safe." He kissed her again then stared deep into her eyes. "I won't do it if you don't want me to, but…" He smiled. "I really think you'll like it."

The gleam in Tal's eyes sent heat simmering through Sonny. It's not that she was afraid of it. She'd learned to turn off her feelings, on some level, during so many sexual acts her captor and his friends had performed on her.

But this was so… personal. So up close and intimate. And all focused on her.

She wasn't quite sure how to receive that type of attention.

But this was Tal. And she could trust him.

She nodded tentatively.

His lips turned up in a broad smile, then he kissed her. His mouth moved on her with such sweet passion, she melted against him, wrapping her arms tightly around his thick, muscular neck.

He drew back, his eyes filled with warmth and awe.

"I love you so much, sweetheart. I can't believe I get to be the one to take your virginity in this."

He kissed slowly down her body. Tingles danced in the wake of his lips. Moving from the base of her neck… down between her breasts… over her stomach. Then he raised his head and gazed at her intimate flesh.

He glanced up at her and smiled, then stroked down her thighs, opening them wider. His focus shifted back to her folds and he glided his thumbs along each side. Then he parted them. His eyes turned dark with need and he leaned forward.

The first touch of his tongue sent an electric pulse of need right through her. He teased over the slick flesh, near her clit but not touching it. His tongue gliding up and down. When it dipped into her opening, she moaned. His tongue was soft, yet firm. And oh, so warm.

It pushed deeper into her and she found herself arching forward. His deep, rumbling laugh against her flesh made her quake with need.

Then she felt the tip of his tongue glide over her clit and she gasped. Warmth spread through her, starting in her core and seeping through every part of her.

He swirled over it. Pleasure spiraled through her. As he continued to lick and cajole her sensitive bud, delightful sensations rippled through her entire body.

"Do you like it, baby?" he asked.

"Oh, yes. Oh, God please—"

Before she could finish her request, he'd found her wet flesh again. His mouth moved on her in what felt like a sweet, intimate, *passionate* kiss… designed so completely for her sole pleasure.

Her fingers wrapped around his head and she held him close, her body writhing beneath him now as pleasure coiled thought her… tighter and tighter…

He suckled on her little button. She arched against him, moaning at the intense joy rippling through her.

"I want you to come for me, baby," he murmured against her burning flesh. Then his tongue swirled over her and plunged inside. He licked, then settled over her clit again.

The tip of his tongue flicked over it, then he sucked on her in small pulses. Her blood turned to liquid fire and her body arched as a thousand suns ignited deep inside her, catapulting her to a state of pure ecstasy. She moaned, her body shuddering as she gave herself over to the blissful surrender.

When her body finally collapsed on the bed, still quivering from the soul-shattering orgasm, he licked and stroked a little longer, continuing the warm glowing pleasure inside her. Then finally his warm mouth drifted away and his body settled beside her, his smiling face next to her on the pillow.

"I hope that was a pleasant first for you."

Her jaw dropped and she stared at him in awe. Then she surged forward, rolling onto her side and capturing his glistening lips. Kissing him deeply. Her tongue glided inside and swirled around. She felt his big, thick cock growing stiffer against her hip.

Her hand found it and she wrapped her fingers around the hard shaft. The heat of it… and the sheer thickness as it pulsed in her hand… had desperate need pulsing through her. Her intimate muscled clenched.

"God, I need you inside me so badly," she said.

He smiled, his whole face lighting up. "Yeah?"

He pressed her onto her back then prowled over her. His body was so muscular. So broad. She drew in a breath as a twinge of panic rippled through her.

"You okay, baby?" he asked, his deep blue eyes penetrating as he searched hers.

She pushed back the lingering ghosts of her past. This was Tal.

Sweet, gentle Tal, who loved her.

She drew in a breath and stroked his cheek as he gazed down at her with concern.

"Yes, Tal. I know I'm safe with you."

His eyes grew fierce and he dipped down and captured her lips.

"Good. I would never do anything to hurt you."

She squeezed his cock, then stroked. It pulsed in her hand, driving her wild with need.

She pressed it to her slick flesh and glided it along her folds, igniting sparks of intense yearning.

"Please, Tal. Fill me."

He chuckled softly and began to move forward. His plump cockhead stretched her as it pushed inside. She opened her legs wider, welcoming his thick shaft into her body.

It glided deeper and deeper. Tingles danced down her spine as his cock stroked her sensitive flesh.

"Ohhhhh, yes. You feel so good inside me."

"Ah, fuck, baby. I can't believe how sweet and warm you feel around me. Gripping me so tightly."

He groaned as his cock filled her the rest of the way. His groin rested tight against her now and the two of them sucked in air as they stared into each other's eyes. His were filled with such potent, poignant desire it took her breath away.

He twitched inside her and she moaned.

She hooked her fingers over his shoulders, clinging to him.

"Oh, God, Tal. I love being this close to you. This intimate. I never thought… after what happened…"

His fingers covered her lips. "Shhh, baby. Don't think about that now. Right now it's just you and me. Sharing this special moment. I'm going to make love to you. I'm going to show you just how much I love you."

She smiled, her eyes welling up. "Yes, Tal. Show me."

He smiled, then keeping his gaze focused on hers, he drew back. Slowly.

Never shifting from his gaze, she whimpered at the sweet sensation of his cock dragging along her inner passage. The delightful feel of it stoking her desire.

His bulging cockhead slid to her opening… almost slipping free… then he surged forward again, filling her in one, smooth stroke.

"Ohhh, Tal."

"Yeah, baby. Do you like the feel of my cock moving inside you?" He drew back, lingering at the edge.

She nodded, tears welling from her eyes at the intensity of the experience.

"Yes." She blinked back the moisture and sighed.

He surged forward again. Pleasure quivered in her core, then expanded through her.

"Oh, God, yes. Fill me."

His nips nuzzled the corner of her mouth. He drew back and drove forward again, making her moan.

His lips turned up in a dazzling smile, the warmth in his eyes searing her.

He started pumping into her, his cock filling her with deep, enthralling strokes. Driving her pleasure higher and higher. She squeezed around him, eliciting a groan so deep and masculine it rippled along her nerve endings, sending her close to the edge.

She clung to his shoulders. "Oh, Tal, I'm so close."

"Yeah, sweetheart." He kissed her lips. "Are you going to come for me?"

He pumped harder. Filling her deeper.

"Oh… yeah…" she panted. "Oh… please."

He pounded into her now. Explosive sensations rippled over her nerve endings. Her insides coiled tighter… tighter… tighter. Then like an overwound spring… released.

She shot over the edge. Catapulting into ecstasy.

"Are you… coming for me… baby?" Tal's words puffed out between thrusts.

She nodded as the orgasm swelled through her, carrying her on a wave of pure bliss.

He laughed as he continued to pump, then he drove deep, shattering her world in and explosion of complete and utterly devastating joy.

She moaned. Long and loud. The sound filling the room with the earthy, primal sound of her release.

"Oh, fuck, baby. You are… so…" His thrusts were faster now. "Fucking… beautiful." He thrust deep, pinning her to the bed. Then he groaned.

Oh, God, she could feel him erupt inside her. Filling her with liquid heat.

She trembled in his arms, moaning. He chuckled against her shoulder, then rocked his hips. She sucked in a breath, then rode the wave as another orgasm swept over her, driven by his cock moving inside her as he kept rocking against her. His lips nuzzling her neck the whole time.

She wailed at the sheer joy embracing her. The bliss he was giving her with his easy movements. The fact he only cared in this moment about her pleasure.

Finally, she collapsed on the bed, panting for air.

"Oh, my God, Tal." She sucked in a breath. "That was… so…"

He laughed, then rolled away, slumping beside her.

"I totally agree." Then he pulled her against him, into the warmth of his embrace.

She sighed, her head against his broad, muscular chest. She nuzzled against it, brushing her lips over one of the tattoos in gentle kisses. Then she rested her head over his heart, listening to its steady beat.

She drew in a deep, contented breath

She could never have imagined being in a man's arms like this after what had happened to her. Especially someone as massive and ultra masculine as Tal. Her fear had been so deeply seated, dug into the far reaches of her soul.

But Tal, with his gentle, protective nature and his deep, sexy voice filled with tenderness and respect, inspired a profound trust in her.

He had brought her back from the abyss and made her whole again.

She stroked her hand over his chest. And she hoped she had done the same for him.

"I love you, Tal," she whispered.

His eyes glowed with happiness as he leaned in and kissed her with a tender brush of his lips.

"And I love you, Sonny."

*I hope you enjoyed **Dirty Talk, Books 3 & 4.***

If you did, please post a review at your favorite online store because that's the best way to help me write more stories like this.

If not, please email me at Opal@OpalCarew.com because I love to hear from my wonderful readers.

Erotic Audios

In this series, Sonny listens to erotic audios Tal makes for her. If you'd like to buy them for yourself, go to **OpalCarew.com/DirtyTalk**

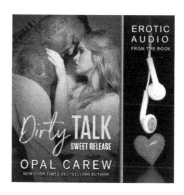

Or you can buy all four erotic audios
as a bundle at
OpalCarew.com/DirtyTalk

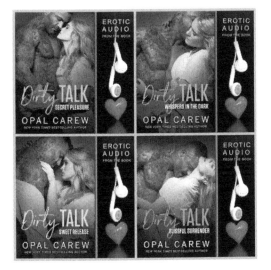

FREE EBOOKS

Would you like more hot, sexy stories?
Join the Opal Carew Reader Group to receive free
erotic reads!
Just go to
OpalCarew.com/ReaderGroup

EXCERPTS

Dirty Talk, Sweet Release and **Dirty Talk, Blissful Surrender** are the final two parts of the **Dirty Talk** series. If you love this narrator (William Martin) as much as I do, you'll also enjoy my **Mastered By** series as audio books, beginning with **Played by the Master**.

If you loved the poignancy of the **Dirty Talk** series, combined with the blazing heat level of the sex scenes, I have a few recommendations as to what to read next...

First is my **Mastered By** series, specifically **Mastered by the CEO**. Rachel is an executive who is just trying to keep her job when her company is taken over, but the new CEO is King Taylor who she used work for and had a relationship with. (Winner of the **National Readers' Choice Award**.)

Second is the stand-alone novella **Debt of Honor**, about a woman who hops off a plane during a refueling stop to search for one-of-a-kind souvenirs, and ends up being held captive by a domineering sheikh in order to pay for a crime she did not commit.

Finally, there is the novel, **Heat**, about a woman whose first love, a firefighter, dies in the line of duty and she vows to keep her heart guarded and never give it away again.

All of the above stories can be found at **OpalCarew.com**

Here are teasers for each story, followed by excerpts...

Mastered by the CEO

Mastered By series

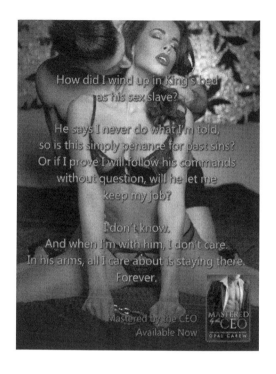

National Readers' Choice Award Winner

Debt of Honor

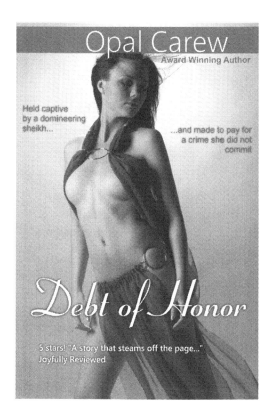

Opal Carew
Award Winning Author

Held captive
by a domineering
sheikh...

...and made to pay for
a crime she did not
commit

Debt of Honor

5 stars! "A story that steams off the page..."
Joyfully Reviewed

Heat

h e a t

opal carew

Thinking about the kiss with Simon
filled her with guilt.
She'd loved Jesse, yet now she
was yearning to let these new men
—two of them no less—kiss her.
Touch her.

To make love to her.

And did you know I also write erotica as Ruby Carew? If you enjoyed **Dirty Talk**, you'll love **Tempting the Boss**...

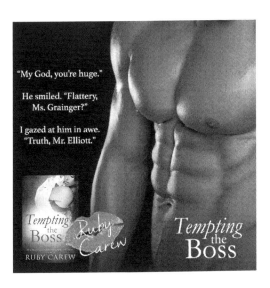

For more about the **Tempting the Boss** series, go to
RubyCarew.com

MASTERED BY THE CEO

OPAL CAREW

Winner of the National Readers' Choice Award

*Rachel knows her job is in trouble when
her ex-lover and boss takes over her company.
Is she willing to totally submit to him—in every way—
in order to prove she'll no longer fight his every
decision?*

Rachel Clark

How did I wind up in King's bed as his sex slave? Being totally dominated by him?

It all started when King bought the company I work for. The last time I was out of work—after handing King my resignation--it took two years before I found another position and I'm desperate to avoid that situation again. So now I'll do whatever I can to keep my job.

But, in fact, even with me submitting to his every whim, there's no guarantee.

King says I'm difficult and never do what I'm told-- which is true—so is this simply penance for past sins? Or if I prove I'll follow his commands without question, will he keep me on?

I don't know. And frankly, I don't care. When I'm in his arms, all I care about is staying there.

Forever.

But that's not an option.

James "King" Taylor

When I bought Bernier Electronics, I didn't know

Rachel was one of the junior executives. With our history, there's no way I can keep her on. I need executives who will do as I say, not constantly question my every move.

I'd like to say it's a difficult decision, but it's not. Our past has proven she won't fit in my management team.

But it's never simple. When she worked for me five years ago, we had a clandestine affair. She insisted on keeping it strictly sexual, but I wanted so much more. When she left, I was devastated. Clearly, it meant more to me than it did to her.

The truth is I still want her in my bed. But I won't hire her just for the sex.

She insists she can change, that she'll do exactly as she's told, but I know that'll never work. Still, offering her the chance to prove herself—by becoming my submissive for an entire weekend—will prove to her it'll never work. I never dominated her when we were together before, and the mere thought has me rock-hard.

I just hope I can handle losing her again after I experience the sweetness of her submission.

Excerpt

King eyed Rachel as she sipped her juice again. He couldn't help watching her full, pouty lips, glistening with juice as she put the glass down. When her pink tongue glided over those lips, his groin tightened.

Her long, chestnut hair was bound at the back of her head with a clip, all the ends neatly tucked in. It was longer than he remembered. Her hair had been too short to put up when they'd worked together, but he'd always told her how he'd love to see her with long hair.

Her eyes, green with specks of gold, remained fixed on her glass. He'd commanded her to be silent and she'd actually obeyed, as much a shock to her, he was sure, as it was to him.

Heat washed through him. He liked the feeling of her following his orders. But then, he'd always known he would.

When she'd called him Mr. Taylor, his heart had leapt. Of course, she always called him that in a professional setting…but here, when they were alone… His heart pounded. If she were to call him Sir, he'd probably burst at the seams.

As he gazed at her now, however, memories of the hot, sensual sessions they'd shared in his office had him longing to hold her in his arms. Longing to feel her naked body against him, her soft sensual murmurs whispering in his ear. To glide his cock deep onto her warm, welcoming body.

His cock swelled, but the band aid on her head reminded him she had a concussion. She was in no condition to even walk straight let alone have wild, savage sex like they used to.

An even deeper craving swelled through him… to do something he'd never done with Rachel. Something he'd yearned to with a force so strong he'd had to hold himself back with an iron fist.

To dominate her. Totally and completely.

But if he'd even tried, he'd been certain she would have run for the hills. Most of the time, she wouldn't even do what he told her as her boss. Trying to command her as his lover… Well, that was doomed to fail.

She lifted her gaze from her glass briefly, then dropped it again when she found he was watching her. At her uncertainty… the slight confusion in her green eyes… protectiveness surged through him.

He loved the fact she needed him right now. Loved that she'd agreed to stay the night so he could watch over her.

The predatory male in him couldn't resist her frailty. Not to take advantage of her, but to take care of her. To know she was his woman and he would protect her.

Even if only for one night.

∼

To buy **Mastered by the CEO** in ebook or audio go to **OpalCarew.com**

DEBT OF HONOR

OPAL CAREW

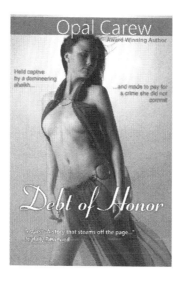

*Detained by an domineering sheikh for a crime she did
not commit...*

Angelica couldn't believe that hopping off a plane during a refueling stop to search for one-of-a-kind souvenirs could lead to so much trouble. Now she is detained in an exotic country by a devastatingly handsome sheikh... and ends up in his harem.

Excerpt

Angelica glanced down at the costume again. It was stunning in royal blue and gold with a gorgeous design formed by the intricate beadwork. The bottom of the bra and the hip band were dripping with beaded fringe. It cascaded from the bra and caressed her bare midriff. She had taken belly dance classes over the past couple of years and had eyed the instructors' costumes, wishing she could afford one for herself, yet this was more exquisite than any she'd ever seen.

"You like it, yes?" one of the women asked. She seemed to be the one in charge.

"It's … beautiful."

The woman took her hand and drew her forward. "Wonderful. The master will be pleased."

Angelica's eyes widened. They were taking her to him in this?

When she slowed down, the women gathered around her and kept her moving forward.

"Stop it. I won't go dressed like this."

"You must. The master has ordered it."

They quickly approached the door. Panic flooded through her. She couldn't.

"I won't wear this!" She reached behind her back and tried to unfasten the bra, but the unfamiliar closure and the fussing hands of the women prevented her from succeeding. She pulled the straps off her shoulders and tried to pull it forward.

"No, miss. You might rip it," one panicked woman insisted.

Rip it. That's exactly what she'd do. She tugged at the straps but they were securely fastened on. She switched to the belt and tugged hard. Despite the women pulling at her arms, she found where it fastened. She realized they had stopped their forward momentum as they struggled with her. She jerked several times until finally, she heard the belt tear, then it fell from her hips.

The women spoke frantically in their own language. Next, she tore at the shimmering, diaphanous fabric of the skirt, ripping it from her body. She shoved her fingertips under the bra beside her left breast and pulled hard. The elastic gave a little and she tried to pull it upwards.

"Stop! You will ruin it."

She felt fingers working at the fastening, then the bra loosened. One of her captors took it, scowling at Angelica.

The woman in charge stepped in front of Angelica, her hands on her hips.

"The master will be very angry."

"Then don't tell him."

"His orders were for you to be brought to him in that outfit."

Angelica placed her hands on her own hips, extremely conscious of her nudity but ignoring it.

"Well, maybe it's time for him to learn that not all his orders will be followed."

One of the women gasped. Angelica suspected the only reason the other woman didn't seem surprised was because she didn't speak English.

She marched away from them, snatched the silk coverlet from the bed and wrapped it around herself. She sat down, her arms crossed over her chest as she held the coverlet firmly around herself.

She had shown them she wouldn't be pushed around, she thought smugly. But Angelica's smugness faded quickly when the women simply dragged her from the bed and led her through the hallways totally naked except for the cover she clung to.

They stopped in front of a heavy wooden door in a tall, arched doorway. The head woman knocked and the door pulled open. A tall guard greeted her and waved them inside. The women led Angelica into a large, sumptuous room filled with plush, upholstered couches and chairs piled high with silk and velvet cushions, all in rich jewel tones, and ornately carved, ebony furniture. They prodded her to the middle of the room and stood behind her. The guard left, but she was certain he would be standing right outside, ensuring she didn't run for it.

"What is this?" a familiar, masculine voice demanded.

She glanced around and saw Kadin, the sinfully gorgeous man who'd insisted she owed him a debt, and demanded she pay with her body. She opened her mouth to voice a protest at her treatment, but his dark, penetrating eyes stole her breath away.

His stormy gaze drifted over the blue silk coverlet cloaking her.

She straightened her shoulders, but tightened her hold on the fabric.

"They refused to provide me with decent clothes."

His eyebrows raised and he stepped toward her. She could read nothing in his coal-black eyes. His mood, whether foul or fair, was a mystery to her. His presence filled the room and, as he approached, she had to force herself not to cringe. Yet at the same time, her body buzzed with an alarming excitement.

Her body reacted to him far too easily. She reminded herself what might happen here tonight. Unfortunately, that kicked the excitement up several notches making her insides quiver.

"I see. So you decided to cover yourself with

this." His tone, low and dangerous, sent alarm skittering through her.

Before she could comprehend what was happening, he grabbed the blanket and yanked it from her grasp.

∽

To buy **Debt of Honor** go to **OpalCarew.com**

HEAT

OPAL CAREW

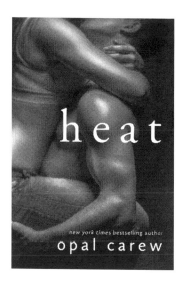

With passion so blazing hot,
you don't want to put this fire out...

When Rikki's first love dies in the line of duty she vows to keep her heart guarded and never give it away again.

After moving to a new town for a fresh start, she is given the opportunity to show off her photography skills and shoot a sexy fireman calendar. Although taking the job might bring up painful memories, she knows this is her best chance at fulfilling her dreams of becoming a professional photographer.

While out with her new roommates, Rikki meets Simon and Carter and feels an instant spark of attraction… to both equally gorgeous and tempting men. This is the same intense feeling she had the first time she fell in love. But how can she feel that way about two men?

When she arrives at the firehouse to shoot the calendar, she is surprised to find that Simon and Carter are firefighters so she immediately pulls back on their growing flirtation. But Simon and Carter are men who know what they want, and they want Riki. As the chemistry between them ignites Rikki finds it hard to resist falling prey to her steamiest fantasies.

Now she has to choose between keeping her heart safe... or taking a chance on love… and possibly losing everything.

Excerpt

As Simon's gaze glided down her body, she realized that wasn't the only thing that was rigid.

God, she wanted him, too. She opened her arms in invitation.

He hesitated only a second, then he surged toward the bed, shedding his clothes on the way. He swooped over her, now naked, and pulled her into his arms, his body tight against her as he kissed her. His tongue pulsed deep and he consumed her like a starving man.

She wrapped her hand around his swollen cock. It was hot and hard. And impossibly thick.

"I want you inside me." Her voice was hoarse and full of need.

He growled, then pressed his cock to her wet folds and thrust inside her. She gasped at his deep penetration.

"Oh, yes!" She nipped his earlobe. "Fuck me."

His blazing midnight eyes seared her senses. Her whole body began to quiver as he drew back. Then he thrust forward again. Filling her deep and hard.

She moaned, clinging to his broad shoulders.

"I'm going to make you come so hard, you'll never forget the feel of me inside you."

Then he thrust deep again. And before she could catch her breath, he thrust again.

He kept pounding into her, as if his life depended on it. Filling her over and over. The intimate stroking of his cock driving her wild with need.

"Oh yes oh yes oh yes," she kept chanting.

She trembled beneath his moving body, accepting every stroke of his cock with wild abandon. Loving the feel of him claiming her so completely.

"Are you close, baby?"

She nodded, unable to utter a word.

"Tell me," he demanded.

She tried and just croaked out a sound as pleasure vibrated through her.

"Tell me!" The command rippled through her, impossible to ignore.

"I'm going to come," she whispered against his ear, already feeling the first wave claiming her.

He thrust harder and she moaned.

"I'm . . . yes . . . Oh, God, I'm . . ." She moaned again. "Coming . . ."

Her voice seemed to vibrate with the pleasure and intensity of the release he was giving her. The orgasm swept over her and tumbled her into bliss. She felt lost in a euphoric swirl of delight.

She could feel her moans pulsing through her body and from her mouth, but the pleasure overrode her sense of time and space. There was only the feel of Simon's cock stroking her deeply. The pleasure rippling through her. And the swell of emotion at being possessed by him.

When he groaned his release, her body jolted

into a new level of hyper pleasure and she lost her hold on reality altogether. Fading into darkness.

∾

To buy **Heat** go to **OpalCarew.com**

TEMPTING THE BOSS

RUBY CAREW

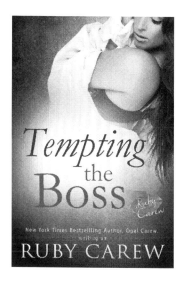

How far will Bella go to keep her job?

Bella loves her job. It's only a temp position but it's
everything she wants in a job... especially her sexy hunk

of a boss. But her hope of being hired at the end of the contract is shattered when he calls her into his office… and tells her she's fired.

Mr. Elliott doesn't want to fire the sexy, and very distracting, Bella, but what else can he do? As much as he might want her to stay, it just isn't working.

Now that the time has come, however, she tempts him with an offer he can't resist. Just how far will she go to keep this job?

Excerpt

I heard the ding of the elevator and glanced at the doors as they whooshed open, revealing Mr. Elliott, gazing at his cell and tapping on the keys. God, he was an exceptionally good-looking man. The moment I'd first seen him, I'd developed an instant crush, which had grown into full-blown, irresistible attraction.

But I'd fought that attraction, knowing that getting involved with the boss was the worst thing I could do. I'd felt it would ruin my chances at a full-time position in the company.

Mr. Elliott glanced up from his phone, then dropped it in his pants pocket as he crossed the reception area. His tailored suit accentuated his broad shoulders, and his square jaw and the subtle shadow of bristle on his chin made him look rugged and extremely masculine.

His steel blue eyes locked onto me, making my breath catch.

"Ms. Grainger. Thank you for staying late to meet with me."

"Of course, Mr. Elliott. It's no problem. I'm usually still here this time of day."

My attempt to impress him with my hard-working attitude seemed to fall on deaf ears as he walked to his office and continued inside, not acknowledging my words.

I stepped into his office and he closed the door behind me, then headed to his executive desk. The big, glossy, mahogany desk was both beautiful and intimidating. A lot like Mr. Elliott himself. There were so many times I'd found myself daydreaming of him calling me into this office and then me walking straight up to him, pulling open my blouse, and begging him to take me right there on that desk.

He sat down and gestured for me to sit in the guest chair facing him. My cheeks flushed at my inappropriate thoughts, hoping he couldn't read them in my face.

But why would he? He'd never shown the slightest interest in me and had no reason to believe I lusted after him.

He grabbed a folder from his desk stand and opened it. After scanning the top paper for a moment, he glanced up. "Ms. Grainger, as you know, your contract with us ends next week."

I drew in a nervous breath.

"Yes, sir. I've enjoyed working here very much." I forced a warm smile, despite the anxiety quivering through me. "I'm hoping that you'll extend my contract so I can continue on here." I gazed at him hopefully. "I was even hoping you might consider me for a full-time position."

But the way he glanced down at the paper in front of him again rather than at me, told me what I needed to know. When he did look me in the eyes, I knew what was coming next.

"I'm sorry, but we will not be extending the contract. Nor hiring you on."

My gut clenched. I knew the department I worked in at Elliott Enterprises was short staffed. I'd heard that they wanted to fill the position with someone full-time and they'd had no luck finding that someone within the company.

"May I ask why, sir?" I asked. "I've worked very hard and I thought you were happy with my work."

His mouth formed a grim line. "I know you have, but I'm sorry, it's just not working out."

Frustration vaulted through me, and my hands tightened into balls. "Have I done something wrong? Is there anything I can do to change your mind?"

I was totally unprepared for the flicker of unadulterated heat in his eyes as his gaze locked on me, but it disappeared so quickly, I began to doubt I'd seen it at all. Still, my insides heated at his interest, even if it was just imagined.

His lips compressed again. "You haven't done anything wrong, but I'm sorry. That's our decision."

Our decision. I knew he had final say on everything that went on in this company, so it was *his* decision.

Unwilling to give up, I pushed it. "You didn't answer me about whether there's anything I can do to change your mind."

Silence hung between us, then he directed his gaze my way. "Like what?"

The opening caught me off guard. "I don't know. Work longer hours? Take on more responsibilities?"

He sighed and closed the folder. "No, I'm afraid not."

I frowned. I'd had his attention enough for him to ask, but what I'd offered hadn't been of interest to him.

Could he be interested in something…different… from me? The thought sent a rush of heat through me, but I knew it must just be my beleaguered imagination acting out.

My fingers tightened around the armrests of my chair. "Mr. Elliott, I really want this job."

"I'm sorry, there are…" He stared at me grimly. "Personality problems."

Shock washed through me. I got along with everyone in the office. I was sure everyone liked me as much as I liked them. Except maybe… his secretary Gina always seemed cool toward me.

"Who?" I asked.

"I don't think it's appropriate to discuss this."

I leaned forward in the chair. "Please, Mr. Elliott. If you're not hiring me because of personality problems, at least tell me what they are, so I don't make the same mistakes at the next place I work."

His fists clenched on his desk. "The problem isn't yours, it's mine," he grated.

Surprise lurched through me. "You don't like me?"

"No, the opposite."

I frowned, confused. "The problem is you *do* like me?"

He stood up, his nostrils flaring. "The problem is, Ms. Grainger, that I'm fucking attracted to you."

I sucked in a breath. "Oh." I certainly hadn't seen that coming.

As his piercing blue eyes locked on me, my body began to tingle with excitement. In disbelief, I realized that not only had he noticed me, he *wanted* me.

His jaw tightened. "I know it's not fair to you, but I find it extremely distracting having you around. And I have a strict policy of not dating employees."

I was dumbfounded. Then a thought occurred to me. "Are you firing me so I won't be an employee and you can ask me out?" I asked almost hopefully.

He gazed at me speculatively. "I assume that wouldn't work."

He didn't wait for my answer. "I know you still have three days left here, but just take tomorrow morning to pass your work off to someone else, and consider the rest of the days as paid vacation.

I drew in a deep breath, not willing to give up on this job yet. He'd just admitted he was attracted to me, and I was definitely attracted to him. I gazed at him and an idea coalesced in my head. It was crazy and brazen, but what did I have to lose?

I stood up and stepped closer to his desk, then leaned forward, my gaze locking on his. "You said you're attracted to me, and that having me around is distracting."

"That's right."

"So what if I find a way to relieve that...*distraction*."

His eyebrows arched. "What do you have in mind?"

My knees felt like rubber as I walked around the big, mahogany desk, determined to convince him to keep me on. I stopped beside his chair, intensely aware of his big, masculine body so close to mine.

"Oh, I think you know," I said calmly.

He turned his chair to face me.

"I'm not sure I do. Why don't you make it crystal clear?" His steel blue gaze challenged me.

Oh, God, could I really do this? I drew in a breath, gathering courage, then crouched in front of him. His legs were parted and I could see a bulge in his pants.

He was turned on. I swallowed. Because of me.

I hesitated, wondering if I should back off. But the thought of actually doing this, of living out the fantasy of being with this man, sent heat thrumming through me.

I rested my hand on his knee, electricity shimmering through me at the contact, then slowly glided up his thigh, over the fine wool of his pants. Excitement skittered through me as my fingers approached the bulge, then slid over it. It thickened as I wrapped my fingers around it, then squeezed.

Oh, God it was so thick and hard.

"Are you suggesting sexual favors in exchange

for me hiring you on?" His voice rumbled from his chest.

"I'm suggesting that if I help relieve your tension, then you won't be so distracted and therefore won't need to let me go." I stroked his shaft. "And it really doesn't seem fair to let me go for something I have no control over."

"So you intend to take control?"

I smiled. "Mr. Elliott, I'm sure you want to be in total control of everything that goes on in your office. I'm just offering you a practical solution to this problem."

I squeezed him again, then stroked and his eyes closed, clearly affected by my attention. Then he opened them and smiled.

"All right. I'll give your idea a chance. Show me what you have in mind."

≈

To buy **Tempting the Boss** go to **RubyCarew.com**

ALSO BY OPAL CAREW

Contemporary erotic short stories & novellas

Taken by Storm (prequel to His to Possess)

Debt of Honor

Dirty Talk series

#1: Dirty Talk, Secret Pleasure

#2: Dirty Talk, Whispers in the Dark

#3: Dirty Talk, Sweet Release

#4: Dirty Talk, Blissful Surrender

Dirty Talk, Books 1 & 2

Dirty Talk, Books 3 & 4

Mastered By series

Played by the Master

Mastered by the Boss

Mastered by my Guardian

Mastered by the CEO

Mastered by her Captor

Mastered by the Sheikh

The Office Slave series

#1: The Office Slave (Red Hot Fantasies #3)

#2: The Boss

#3: On Her Knees

#4: Her New Master

#5: Please, Master

#6: Yes, Sir

#7: On His Knees

The Office Slave Series, Book 1 & 2

The Office Slave Series, Book 3 & 4

The Office Slave Series, Book 5 & 6

The Office Slave Series, Book 7 & Bonus

Red Hot Fantasies series

#1: The Male Stripper

#2: The Stranger

#3: The Office Slave

#4: The Captive (prequel to Mastered by her Captor)

#5: The Bridal Affair

Red Hot Fantasies, Volume 1 (Books 1-3)

Red Hot Fantasies, Volume 2 (Books 4-5)

Ready To Ride biker series

Hot Ride

Wild Ride

Riding Steele (novel)

Hard Ride (novel)

Ready to Ride, Book 1 & 2

Three series

#1: Three

#2: Three Men and a Bride

#3: Three Secrets

Three Happy Endings (Books 1-3)

Futuristic erotic romance novellas

Slaves of Love

Abducted series

formerly Celestial Soul-Mates series

#1: Forbidden Mate

#2: Unwilling Mate

#3: Rebel Mate

#4: Illicit Mate

#5: Captive Mate

Fantasy erotic romance

Crystal Genie

Contemporary erotic romance novels

A Fare To Remember

Nailed

My Best Friend's Stepfather

Stepbrother, Mine

Hard Ride

Riding Steele

His To Claim

His To Possess

His To Command

Illicit

Insatiable

Secret Weapon

Total Abandon

Pleasure Bound

Bliss

Forbidden Heat

Secret Ties

Six

Blush

Swing

Twin Fantasies

Contemporary erotic romance (ebook only)

Meat

Big Package

Drilled

Collections and Anthologies

Dirty Talk, Books 1 & 2

Dirty Talk, Books 3 & 4

The Office Slave Series, Book 1 & 2

The Office Slave Series, Book 3 & 4

The Office Slave Series, Book 5 & 6

The Office Slave Series, Book 7 & Bonus

Red Hot Fantasies, Volume 1 (Books 1-3)

Red Hot Fantasies, Volume 2 (Books 4-5)

Ready to Ride, Book 1 & 2

Three Happy Endings (Books 1-3)

Turn Up The Heat (anthology) – contains Slaves of Love

Northern Heat (anthology) – contains Three

◦⁓◦

ALSO BY RUBY CAREW

Contemporary erotic short story series

Jenna's Best Friend's Father series

#1: Jenna's Punishment

#2: Jenna's Two Masters

Jenna's Best Friend's Father - Collection 1

Tempting the Boss series

#1: Tempting the Boss

#2: Tempting the Boss, The Arrangement

#3: Tempting the Boss, Obsessed

#4: Tempting the Boss, The New Partner

Tempting the Boss - Collection 1

Tempting the Boss - Collection 2

All He Wants series

#1: All He Wants: For Christmas Eve

#2: All He Wants: For Christmas

All He Wants – Christmas Collection

ABOUT THE AUTHOR

As a *New York Times* and *USA Today* bestselling author of erotic contemporary romance, Opal Carew's books have won several awards, including the National Readers' Choice Award (twice), the Golden Leaf Award (twice), the Golden Quill (3 times), CRA Award of Excellence, and Silken Sands.

Opal writes about passion, love, and taking risks. Her heroines follow their hearts and push past the fear that stops them from realizing their dreams… to the excitement and love of happily-ever-after.

Opal loves nail polish, cats, crystals, dragons, feathers, pink hair, the occult, Manga artwork, Zentangle, and all that glitters. She grew up in Toronto, and now lives in Ottawa with her husband, huge nail polish collection, and five cats.

One of her sons just finished his second Masters degree in Geopolitics (first at Sussex University in the UK and second at Carleton University in Ottawa.) The other son has an undergraduate degree from Carleton University and is now working at Apple. Yes, mom is proud!

To keep in touch with Opal, you can contact her at Opal@OpalCarew.com or use the social media links below:

- Reader Group: OpalCarew.com/ReaderGroup
- Website: OpalCarew.com
- Facebook: OpalCarewRomanceAuthor
- Twitter: @OpalCarew
- Pinterest: opalcarew
- Tumbler: opalcarew.tumblr.com
- Blog: bit.ly/OpalsBlog
- Goodreads: bit.ly/OC_Goodreads
- Contact Opal: bit.ly/contactopal

Made in the USA
Monee, IL
10 January 2020